Twelve Travelers, Twenty Horses

BOOKS BY HARRIETTE GILLEM ROBINET

Ride the Red Cycle

Children of the Fire

Mississippi Chariot

If You Please, President Lincoln

Washington City Is Burning

The Twins, the Pirates, and the Battle of the New Orleans

Forty Acres and Maybe a Mule

Walking to the Bus-Rider Blues

Missing from Haymarket Square

Twelve Travelers, Twenty Horses

Twelve Travelers, Twenty Horses

Harriette Gillem Robinet

ATHENEUM BOOKS FOR YOUNG READERS
New York London Toronto Sydney Singapore

ATHENEUM BOOKS FOR YOUNG READERS
An imprint of Simon & Schuster Children's Publishing Division
1230 Avenue of the Americas, New York, New York 10020
Copyright © 2003 by Harriette Gillem Robinet
Map drawn by Rick Britton
Book design by O'Lanso Gabbidon
The text of the book is set in Bembo.
Printed in the United States of America
First Edition
2 4 6 8 10 9 7 5 3 1
Library of Congress Cataloging-in-Publication Data
Robinet, Harriette
Twelve travelers, twenty horses / Harriette Gillem Robinet.
p.   cm.
Summary: On the way to California with their kind new master,
thirteen-year-old Jacob, his mother, and other slaves are caught up in
adventures that include trying to stop a plot to help the South secede
from the Union.
ISBN 0-689-84561-8
1. African Americans—Juvenile fiction. [1. African Americans—Fiction.
2. Slavery—Fiction. 3. Adventure and adventurers—Fiction. 4. West
(U.S.)—Fiction. 5. United States-History—1849-1877—Fiction.] I. Title.
PZ7.R553   Tu 2003
[Fic]—dc21   2001053667

I wish to thank Emily Howald who assisted me with understanding horses and corrected my mistakes. She learned about horses from her late husband, George James. Emily and George's horses, used for trail riding, were the following Missouri Fox Trotters: a white mare named Peppermint Patty, and a chestnut gelding named Mo.

Their palomino colt, named George's Golden Pride and born after George died, was bred from a bay mare named Becky Thatcher and a palomino stallion named Lad.

I wish to thank the adults and children of Lexington Christian Academy of Lexington, Kentucky. Thank you for your inspiration and hospitality; thank you for the tour of Calumet Horse Farm.

I also wish to thank the librarians at our Oak Park, Illinois, library who are always kind in providing for my research.

Twelve Travelers, Twenty Horses

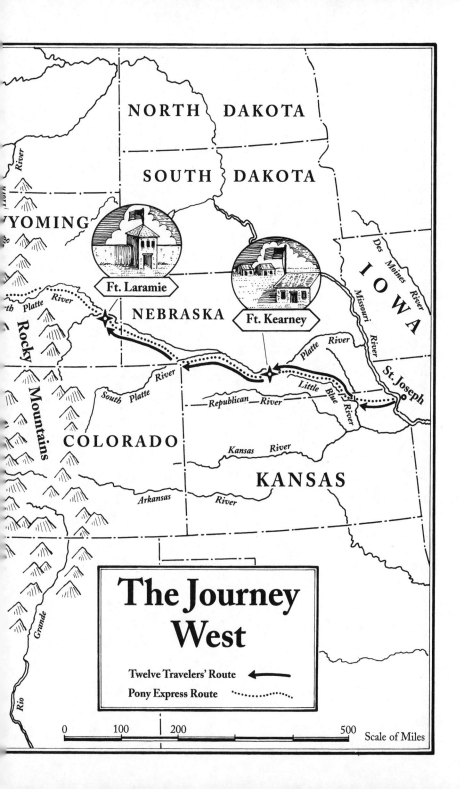

1

Pink and yellow maple leaves made light of the September of 1860 in Kentucky, where I lived. I was an American boy of African ancestry; I was also a thirteen-year-old slave.

For us slaves, the United States was taking turns blowing cold blasts to drive us to despair and warm gusts to help us hope. When would we be free?

The times gave us to understand that the November elections of 1860 would determine which way our lives would go. Voters would decide between Republican Mr. Abraham Lincoln or one of the three Democrats in the presidential race, including Mr. Stephen Douglas.

That week in September, Solomon, who was nine years old, Caesar, who was twenty years old, and I walked barefoot in chains on cold roads to be sold at auction. Along the way the salesmen added more slaves to our number, until we were shackled to about fifteen other men and boys.

At the auction house they kept us bound, lying on benches in the dark. The chains made me furious, and I felt humiliated. They caged my body in rusty iron, but my soul burned as a flame in the night.

Finally on the morning of the sale they removed my chains. They made me stand naked while they washed me with buckets of cold water. With a hand-size slab of pork fat, they greased my body until I shone. I dressed myself. The only reason I endured was because I had earned this sale, and I was proud of it.

They fed me well that morning, bacon rinds and corn bread. It wouldn't do for the auctioneer to have a slave faint on the auction block just as the bidding got good.

I was blinded as I stumbled out into bright light. The sun was almost at noon as we walked to a grassy commons. Salesmen hawked us and other white people sneered at us. Buyers called us stupid, ugly, black face.

Although I looked at the grass as if I be ashamed, I wasn't. I felt sorry for them white folks. My mama had taught me that we were all equal children of the earth and loved by our creator.

We stood, some seventy-five "prize Negro slaves," barefoot in cold grass that smelled newly cut. The auctioneer said he never held a sale until he had at least seventy-five slaves. That's how I knew how many we were.

I wore a brown suit and a white shirt. We were dressed in showy clothes, which the auctioneers usually took back after we were bought. This was my third time being sold, and I had an understanding about auctions.

I searched for Solomon and spied him standing alone. When I walked near, he backed toward me. He was smart in some ways. We were free to move around now, but men with guns patrolled us. Any slave making a fast move to escape would be shot in a second. Big Caesar bumped my shoulder, but we didn't look at each other. No one must know that we were friends, because friends were always sold separately.

However, when Solomon started to rock and play with his fingers in front of this face, I held his hands down. Even so, he would never be sold. Who would buy poor Solomon? He was nine and as tall as me, but he had never uttered a word. Allow me to add that I was short for my age.

Reunited with Caesar and Solomon, I relaxed and looked around. We were being sold on a green commons in front of a redbrick courthouse of American justice. That fact brought tears to my eyes.

Solomon grew restless and pulled his hands free. He mustn't show how he was in the head. I knew how to make him stop. I whispered, "Stay still for the butterfly."

Solomon would stand for hours watching butterflies. He stared at the ground waiting. There weren't any flowers nearby, but the last butterfly of summer flitted past. As we watched the orange and brown butterfly sail off, who should I see among the slaves but mama.

I trembled in excitement. It had been three years since I last saw Eliza, my mama. I had thought that I would never see her again.

She hadn't noticed me, so I held Solomon by his hands and slowly stepped toward her. She caught sight of me, covered her mouth, and began silent crying. Tears rolled down my face too.

I had found Mama, my Eliza, after all these years. The last time I was sold, I had left her weeping on the auction block. Now we were together again, if only for a few minutes.

We dared not hug, but stood shoulder to shoulder. She wiped her eyes to stopping. When she squeezed them tight, I knew Mama was praying, thanking the Lord.

Caesar must have suspected that Eliza be my mama. Moving behind me, he squeezed my shoulder. For the past three years Big Caesar had taken care of me like a brother. He stood over six feet tall, and I heard tell he was over two hundred pounds. His voice was as deep as he was big. Like me, he was an honest worker, but Master sold us for setting fire to his barn.

Master had said, "I feel like shooting you two on the spot, but I ain't losing no money. The times are tight. You were both caught running away and now caught setting fires. You're off to be sold."

Since I had kept Solomon around me working at the Big House, Master had got rid of him along with Caesar and me. Although Solomon had been born on the master's plantation, his mother was dead; no one wanted a boy like him.

I heard a soft grunt, and Milo bumped me. I hadn't seen him in three years either. Eliza and Milo had been sold together again. Imagine meeting people I loved.

Milo was a team driver, about ten years older than Eliza. If she be thirty now, he must have been forty. They said he had hands like silk for mules or horses. Medium in size, he had a good heart and a bad habit: Milo gambled.

One New Year's Eve, I heard tell he lost all his clothes to gambling. He would have gone bare bottom and freezing cold if somebody hadn't shared a shirt and pants.

Next, when I looked over my shoulder, Kentucky Bob stood by us. He was fair of skin, with shoulder-length, straight brown hair, and was about thirty-five years of age. A curved scar, like a new moon, marked his pale tan face from forehead to chin.

In the neighboring county they said he was a violent man, quick to fight and sure to win. He had an angry eye, that Kentucky Bob. If I hadn't been leaning against Eliza, I would have moved away. I didn't take to trouble lessen trouble took to me.

Someone stepped on my bare toes to get my attention. It was Chloe, who lived on the horse farm next to Master's plantation. Slaves from both farms attended church services together in the fields. I reckoned she was about my age. Her black hair was braided in neat cornrows. For the sale she wore a pink dress that made her round face glow. We had never said more than a word or two to each other, but I had heard good things about Chloe.

Seth followed Chloe. Because they looked alike, I figured he was her older brother, about twenty years old, like Caesar. He sang at church services in a voice like honey, and I remembered hearing about how his wife and child had died in birthing.

Seth was always protecting black womenfolk and getting in trouble with the masters for it. He was a decent man. Polly, the cook, wearing her red turban, and Hannah, the midwife and tender to the sick, followed behind Seth.

Those four—Chloe, Seth, Polly, and Hannah—were all from the neighboring horse farm, and I wondered why they were being sold. This was like a dream, meeting with Mama and friends.

All of us were dark—coffee brown of skin—except for Kentucky Bob and Hannah, who were cream-colored. The cook, Polly, and Hannah, the midwife, were older than Eliza, maybe in their forties, like Milo.

When Solomon again began to rock and hold his fingers in front of his face, Polly and Hannah took his hands. I guess all the slaves in the county knew about Solomon.

Poor Solomon. For three years I had taken care of him.

I hated to think that we would be separated. What did they do with wrong-in-the-head slaves no one wanted to buy? It made me shudder.

Eliza felt me tremble and leaned closer. Tears welled in my eyes. It was so good to be by my mama. We stood in the middle of a group of slaves drawn together, I decided, by a kind of longing. My heart was full, my soul was singing. I took a deep breath and raised my eyes to heaven.

A maple with pink leaves laughed in the breeze, and golden oaks rustled giggles in reply. The noonday sun was high and glorious over seventy-five people about to be sold.

The open sky was free, but we were ten shivering slaves: Jacob, that be me; Eliza, my mama; Big Caesar, my friend; Solomon, the needy; Milo, the team driver; Kentucky Bob, the violent; Seth, the protector; Chloe, Seth's sister; Polly, the cook; and Hannah, the healer. Ten of us, I counted. Three children: Jacob, Chloe, and Solomon. Seven grown-ups. Aching needs held us together.

The slave auction hadn't yet begun when a young, rosy-faced white man no more than twenty, like Caesar and Seth, with bronze brown hair and brown eyes, walked over to us grinning. At first I thought he was a simpleton. His stovepipe hat was too big for him and sat loosely tilting on his ears.

Dressed like a dandy, he wore a black, cutaway frock coat showing a gray vest. Although it was hardly that cold, he wore gray spats over his shiny shoes and black leather gloves.

The white man strutted up and down in front of us. He was probably selecting slaves, but he seemed ashamed to examine us. Buyers often squeezed our arms and legs for muscles. Kentucky Bob's lip raised in a sneer. I hoped he wouldn't say anything, but Kentucky whispered, "Dang fool," into a breeze.

Stovepipe Hat seemed embarrassed about buying slaves. But that was better than the white man nearby who made an old woman run around in a circle, then pried open her mouth to tap on her teeth.

For a second Eliza held my hand, then let go. These might be our last moments. Could we ever be together again? Closing my eyes, I dared not ask God. It was enough that I could be near Eliza for a few minutes. I knew she was still alive. My beloved mama.

Caesar bumped my shoulder. When I opened my eyes, I saw Stovepipe Hat walking over with a salesman. Stovepipe seemed so young, maybe nineteen or twenty. Did this white man have money?

"How much for all ten of these fine slaves?" Stovepipe Hat asked.

Mama squeezed her eyes shut, Milo hissed softly, and Kentucky Bob gave a soft snort. I almost laughed. The auction hadn't begun yet, and this young master hadn't noticed Solomon. I squeezed Solomon's hands.

Ordinarily at that time a man-slave cost from one thousand to eighteen hundred dollars and women cost five to eight hundred, depending on age. Children cost three or four hundred, according to health and size.

Stovepipe Hat stood with arms open. What kind of slave buyer was he? He hadn't made us walk or run or jump. He hadn't squeezed our muscles or looked at our teeth. And what about Solomon?

Next the young master told the salesman, "I'm a very rich man, I'll have you understand."

Didn't Stovepipe Hat see the greedy grin on that salesman's face? Masters never told when they were wealthy. What a way to bargain!

"How about two thousand each?" said the salesman.

"Sold," said our new master.

2

After the sale was completed—money paid and papers passed—men stripped us of the sales clothes. A clock in the courthouse rang one o'clock with a big boom. Arms folded, our young master gazed at us grinning. Caesar, Seth, and Kentucky Bob towered over the man, stovepipe hat and all. Milo, Solomon, and I were near his size.

He told us: "Men and women of labor, I am your new owner. The name is the Honorable Mister Clarence Higgin"—he paused—"Higginboom!"

He actually bowed to us. Caesar and I led the others in bowing back to him. Some men buying slaves nearby laughed, but Eliza was whispering, "Praise the Lord. I be with my child, Jacob Israel!"

Kentucky Bob said in a low voice, "Dang fool. First white person ever called me a man." He sounded disgusted; he was angry about being treated with respect. Maybe this was a new kind of master. Maybe Stovepipe Hat wasn't a simpleton after all. I shook my head.

Polly, the cook, sighed. "What blessings flow," she said. "The Lord is good," whispered Hannah, the healer.

Taking a deep breath, I stared at the white man. He had called us men and women, had paid an enormous price for us. Who was this man, or boy? Now what? We stood shyly staring at him, but he didn't scold us. Most masters insisted that slaves bow their heads and look at the ground. Already I felt bolder.

The new master went on: "Allow me to say, or have I said it to you? Anyway, I am a very, very wealthy man." He tried to adjust his hat; he strutted back and forth in front of us. "Rich, you hear?"

A chilly breeze ruffled the leaves and blew Chloe's torn petticoat. We stood shivering in clean but ragged underwear.

"Now, to prove it," said our young master, "follow me. I'll buy all of you new clothes." As he started to walk away he glanced over his shoulder at our bare feet. "And shoes," he called.

We were free to follow him along a wooden sidewalk. No one behind us. No one in front. No chains. No men with rifles walking alongside.

Kentucky Bob said, "No need running, I can walk away from this fool." He added, "I be just staying for clothes and shoes."

Milo said, "Ain't nobody more stupid than a man with new money. Old money makes misers; new money makes fools."

Meek as hungry kittens, we followed the master across town to a street of merchants. All afternoon shopkeepers fitted us out in ready-made clothes. The ten of us were dressed like free women and men in clothes of our choice. We even carried new winter underwear.

I received a fine, cold-weather outfit, including knit socks, high-top leather shoes with growing room, and a blue plaid cap. I wore a gray, wool-tweed suit and a blue flannel shirt. My scratchy new clothes smelled wonderfully store-bought.

When we walked out of the last shop, I felt someone had to say something, so I said: "Thank you, Master."

"You will not call me Master," he said. "Men and women of labor, listen to me." Like a preacher, he raised both arms as he stood in front of us gathered outside that store. "I am the Honorable Mister Higginboom. You can call me Honorable Mister."

Covering my mouth, I controlled my giggle. This master was funny, and I felt dizzy from happiness. I had Mama, good friends, and warm clothes. Wind blew dust and dry leaves down that Kentucky street. Just then the shopkeeper backed out of his store, locking the door for the night. There was a brief sunset flare of cloud-flowing beauty, and darkness descended.

Chloe followed my lead. "Thank you, Honorable Mister."

The young master grinned. "The title rings like a

church bell, don't it?" he said. "Now to our inn for food and bedding, men and women. Follow me."

He trotted off down the street.

"Follow him to the inn," Milo said. "What inn? Under what horse in the barn do I sleep? Want to bet?"

"Barn," said Seth.

"Inn," I said to be contrary.

Eliza said, "Inn kitchen by the fire, I hope."

Polly, Hannah, and Chloe said, "Barn."

Caesar and Kentucky Bob grunted, but Solomon bent back and forth playing with his fingers.

Now Seth began whispering to Polly, the cook, and Hannah, the healer, about running away with him and Chloe. The streets were dark, and he knew, as we did, that there were forests all around that frontier town.

Eliza told Seth, "Why don't you eat first? Get the feeling of the slave work?"

"And when he hire himself an overseer, we never get this chance again," said Kentucky Bob. "I be leaving now. Look at that fool man. He ain't even looking back."

That was true. I moved to the front of the group to get away from Kentucky Bob and saw that Honorable Mister was half a block ahead of us. That was amazing. I was glad that Eliza wasn't for running. I didn't want to lose her, and laws were bad now.

Because of Dred Scott's case, couldn't nobody run without being caught again and made a slave, even in a so-called free state. And I heard California's Compromise brought back the Fugitive Slave Laws. For white people, there were penalties for helping slaves escape north and punishment for not capturing a runaway slave.

Two years ago Caesar and I had made it running away from Kentucky through Indiana and into Illinois. But we were caught by bounty hunters and returned to Master's whipping post. I had thought I would die from that beating for sure. And now because of setting the fire, we were sold. However, I had been at slave auctions before.

My first sale was with Eliza when I was a one-year-old and our master had died. We were sold as part and parcel of his estate. When I was six, Eliza and I—with the help of some Quakers—had made it all the way to Boston in bales of hay. For almost four years we had been free. She worked as a dressmaker; I attended school and learned to read and write and cipher.

Then one night bounty hunters kidnapped us, drove us south tied and gagged in a wagon, and sold us to slave auction men in Virginia. That had been my second sale when I was about ten years old. Today had been my third.

Slaves who had been with one master in one place all their lives didn't know about the Constitution and the courts. I did. I sneaked books and newspapers from Master to read in secret. Because courts had abolished slavery in Massachusetts, Eliza and I had tasted freedom there; but we had been taken captive and sold back into slavery.

I had thought it would be the death of Eliza, she took the return so hard. Waiting to be sold, she had stared into space, spoke in a weak voice, and hardly moved.

As for me, I had cried for a while, but I had been confused: Was I born to be a slave? Only later did I realize that no one was ever meant to be a slave. Now freedom was in the air.

I wasn't for running, neither I nor Caesar. Seemed from what she said, Eliza wasn't for escaping either.

Chloe trotted up beside me. "You aiming to run too?"

"Not me," I said.

"Not me either," she said. "Besides, did you hear about Mr. Abraham Lincoln?"

"I know," I said, smiling.

"If he wins he'll be the first president the Republicans ever had," she said, "and election be in November. If they vote for Mr. Lincoln as president, they say we be as good as free."

I added: "Besides freedom for slaves, they say there're winds of war a-blowing if Mr. Lincoln be elected. But if one of the three Democrats wins, slavery will be in the North and West, as well as in the South."

Chloe nodded. "Jacob, you read the papers too!"

"I can read."

"So can I." So Chloe was educated. Not many slaves knew how to read and write. In fact, it was against the law to teach a slave to read.

As we hurried along the street I glanced at Chloe. How pretty she looked. She wore the new broadcloth dress dyed blue, a black shawl with fancy fringes, and a short blue bonnet tied under her chin. Across the street two white women walked in plain, unbleached, cotton dresses. Thanks to Honorable Mister, we slaves were dressed fine and fancy.

Suddenly I thought about Solomon. I looked around. Where was he? "Help me find Solomon," I told Chloe, and I walked back.

Most of the time Solomon couldn't take care of himself. In new surroundings he needed someone to guide him, but he was smarter than most people thought.

Once the roof on our slave cabin was loose, and we needed to fasten it down. I had put stones on to hold it, but wind and rain washed them off, and we were wet sleeping. Caesar had tried too, but nothing he did helped. Late one night Solomon woke me.

When I sat up, he pushed a hammer and four nails into my hand. After Caesar nailed the roof, Solomon disappeared with the hammer. Later I saw it back among our master's tools.

Now, how did Solomon know to borrow it?

As I searched for him Eliza caught my hand. "We ain't had time to talk, Jacob Israel."

"We'll talk, Mama."

"Not Mama, call me Eliza, son. Don't let on to the

Honorable Mister that we're kin, or it'll be used to hurt us, sure as I breathe. But thank the Lord we be together again."

"Yes," and I hugged her. "Have you seen Solomon?"

"Why you holding on to him, Jacob? You should take care of yourself. You be always minding somebody else's business."

"I take care of myself, I do, Eliza." I had almost called her Mama. Once I had called her Mama every day. We had lived over the dressmaking shop where she had sewed infant wardrobes for an English shopkeeper.

"Eliza, you see how Solomon be."

"God take care of fools and babies, Jacob Israel."

Chloe ran up to me. "He not be here."

"Probably still standing by the store," I said, and we ran back, but I felt strange leaving the group. I hadn't asked permission, because Honorable Mister was too far away.

Two blocks back Solomon stood on the wooden side-walk rocking back and forth in front of the last store.

"Solomon," I shouted. He stopped rocking. By the lantern light of a passing carriage, I saw him smile like the flicker when a candle's blown out. Then his face went blank again. That was Solomon.

Chloe and I returned, dragging him between us. We hastened to catch up with the others, and I was panting with fear. I loved our little group, Mama and the others. Suppose the new master grew angry with me and returned me for sale?

Finally we saw the other slaves standing by a bonfire. Kentucky Bob and Seth were among them; we slaves were still together. I felt relief wash over me like warm rain.

A man seemed to be arguing with our new master. The man shook his clenched fists. Who was this man? Our Honorable Mister Higginboom was being called Higgins. What was his name, anyway?

3

"Where's my money, Higgins?" yelled the heavyset man. "You're nothing but a humbug, a scoundrel, and a rascal!"

Our Honorable Mister held his stovepipe hat and tried to explain something. As the bonfire crackled and burned it made leaping shadows and smelled of smoky pinewood. A crowd had gathered to watch.

Chloe, Solomon, and I ran up to the rear where the women were. Eliza jerked my hand off Solomon's and pushed me forward. She always wanted me to speak up, to take action. I remembered that. I wormed myself through the crowd to the front until I stood with Milo and Seth just behind Kentucky Bob and Caesar.

"Zeke paid you for them oxen, Sam. I ain't owing you nothing."

"And where is Zeke Hill? Tell me that?" the man yelled.

"Told you before, Zeke died natural from a fall off a cliff. But he paid you for all that outfit."

As they fussed back and forth I wondered why the Honorable Mister didn't just give this Sam some money. He said he was rich. Somehow I felt sorry for the young master, and I felt grateful for my clothes and shoes.

"Murderer! I heard from the camp, Higgins. You murdered Zeke Hill for his gold, now didn't you?" The man clutched Honorable's arm with one hand and raised his fist to hit him. Our new master dropped his hat.

What did that man mean calling our new master a murderer?

Eliza wanted me to do something. I tapped Big Caesar; he turned to Kentucky Bob. Without a word, they stepped into the circle of firelight and grabbed the man, Sam, lifting him by his arms and shoulders off the street. For a moment I thought Kentucky Bob would throw the man into the fire, but he didn't. He and Caesar held him near the flames, though.

Firelight seemed to widen the moment. People in the crowd backed away. The Honorable Mister stooped slowly and put on his stovepipe hat. He tried to straighten it, but it covered his eyebrows and tilted back and forth on his ears. Why hadn't he bought a hat that fit him? Standing beside him, I saw his grin.

"Sam, me and my people of labor are going now. You been paid; Zeke's been buried; and my name is Higginboom. A classy name, Higginboom. You hear that? The Honorable Mister Clarence Higginboom."

He strutted off, leaving Sam in Kentucky Bob's and Caesar's hands. I saw them grin and shrug at each other like friends, but they were so different. Caesar was peaceful, and Kentucky Bob had a reputation for violence.

Chloe ran up beside me with Solomon safe in hand. We both smiled because we knew what the men wanted to do with that Sam. Although Milo said our new master was a fool with new money, I liked this Honorable Mister.

Somehow I wanted to protect him. I was a boy, and he was young too. We slaves had taken sides, but we didn't really know who was right. Besides, Sam had called our new master a murderer. That bothered me.

Milo waved us to follow Honorable Mister. Eliza walked beside him. Seth took Polly and Hannah by their shawl-covered shoulders and beckoned to Chloe. But she stayed by me.

The bonfire was warm, and the light made Chloe's face shine. I turned to the men by the smoky fire. When Caesar looked from Kentucky Bob to me, I said, "Put him down gentle like." But who was I to tell them?

Sam's face was whiter than the moon, and he stood watching us walk off. I heard him say, "I'll get that Higgins. That scoundrel is part of them conspirators. I'll tell Washington about the Knights of the Golden Circle."

That sounded interesting. Knights of the Golden Circle?

As we walked Chloe said, "Wasn't that something? But I didn't be scared. I wasn't much afraid at the auction, neither. Do you know how we happened to get sold? Me, Hannah, Polly, and Seth?"

"No." I had wondered about it.

"It was so fast, no one in the county could pass word. I had heard that you and Caesar be sold. And I be so proud that you set fire to that barn."

I nodded. I was pleased about the fire too, and I'd do it again in two shakes of a puppy dog's tail. Leaving friends on the plantation had been difficult, but I was reunited with Mama, Milo, Caesar, and Solomon.

"Well, Master had a son about sixteen, you know. And he kept whistling for me to come to him. Polly told me never to answer him. She said that St. Paul say, 'You be the temple of God, and the Spirit of God live in you.' That made me care for myself.

"So," continued Chloe, "one day when I be gathering eggs, that boy be hiding in the henhouse. He caught me and tried to kiss me."

I frowned and shook my head. Not Chloe!

"He held my arms down, and I was too close to kick him like Hannah kicks men. So I bit his lip bleeding to his chin."

She grinned. "How that boy screamed! Polly had been gathering sage for chicken soup. When she heard him yelling, she ran to the henhouse and hit him with a rake. She told him, 'Don't you never touch Chloe again.'

"Hannah bound up his lip and warned him she'd get him. And then Seth sent word he was looking for him.

"Next morning the slave wagon rolled by, and Master sold all four of us: Polly, Hannah, Seth, and me. I miss the other slaves, but I be so happy to get rid of that boy." She smiled.

At that moment my Book of Life opened to the page of who I would marry, and I wrote Chloe's name. I looked up at the night sky, and my heart sang, hallelujah!

At the inn the keeper fed us in a separate room with the Honorable Mister. I think Kentucky Bob and Seth were glad they hadn't run yet. We ate good-smelling lamb stew with plenty of carrots and potatoes, as many helpings as we wanted. Then our new master ordered a slice of sweet apple pie for each of us, even for Solomon.

Never had I eaten anything as good as that pie. I hadn't tasted apple pie before, but I had smelled pies cooking in the Big House kitchen.

I won Milo's bet. We slept at the inn, men in one room and women in another. Those who couldn't share beds slept on the floor. Never having slept in a bed, I slept on the floor with Solomon. But I smelled the sweet hay in the men's mattresses.

Honorable had his bed in the room with his men slaves. If he had known Kentucky Bob's reputation, our young master wouldn't have snored so peacefully.

Milo said, "It be a sure bet this white boy ain't never

been around slaves before." A master trusting his "men and women of labor," as Honorable put it, was unheard of.

After the candle was blown out and before I went to sleep, I patted down Solomon. He had a way of taking things—hats, scarfs, candlesnuffers, tools—and then I had to return them.

The next day the Honorable Mister Higginboom handed us blue blankets of well-woven wool and rode with us on a stagecoach going to Missouri. In the coach were two long benches that seated four or five people each, along with a single seat. Of course, the women and our new master rode inside, so Caesar and me took a turn sitting outside with the driver.

Before we left Kentucky, we drove past a group of people who were carrying signs and singing. As soon as I heard Lincoln's name I tapped on the coach for Chloe and Eliza. Chloe stuck her head out the window.

They sang:

> *"Old Abe Lincoln came out of the wilderness,*
> *Out of the wilderness, out of the wilderness,*
> *Old Abe Lincoln came out of the wilderness,*
> *Down in Illinois."*

Up until then our stagecoach driver had held his tongue; I don't think he took a liking to sitting with two slaves. But he spoke when we passed the singers.

"And Kentucky will send Lincoln back to the wilderness," he said with a grunt. "Them Wide Awakes want to plunge the States into war. Mr. John Bell will win." He muttered a few other words, then said, "I seen him. That Abe Lincoln's a country bumpkin, too tall for his britches."

Holding on to the swaying coach, I looked back. What exciting times. Mr. Lincoln was our breath of hope from slavery's suffocation. Eliza and Chloe nodded out the window before closing it.

How that team of six horses trotted! The roads were dry, the trees were red and gold, and crisp fall leaves flew with the crows. Every fifty miles the stagecoach changed horses, and every one hundred miles it changed drivers.

Milo and Kentucky Bob took turns with me and Caesar riding outside.

Milo said, "That driver's good. With a well-trained team of horses, you need be starting them and stopping them. Otherwise, you let them horses trot the roads at their own speed."

For four or five days at inns we were treated like citizens, not slaves. The Honorable Mister Clarence Higginboom ordered the best of everything for us.

"He's just showing off how rich he be," said Milo one evening.

Hannah told him, "The young master might be gentle, you know. There be kind white people."

"He's a dang fool," said Kentucky Bob.

Honorable wouldn't let anyone drink ale, however. "No hard drink, men of labor," he told us. "My partner almost lost our fortune because of whiskey." He patted his head. "I may be young, but I know to stay sober."

One night we men sat at a table together across the dining room from the women's table. When Honorable left to talk to the innkeeper, Milo leaned forward.

"Want to bet on the Honorable Mister?" he said.

"What're you betting?" I asked.

"Your pie tomorrow night."

We had had mincemeat pie—warm apples and raisins—that night. And Eliza had warned me never to bet with Milo.

"Sure," I said.

"I bet he wears gloves because he's missing a finger."

Now, we had all wondered. The last thing our new master took off at night and the first thing he put on in the morning were those black leather gloves. He even ate in them.

I figured Milo had seen his hand. "No fair betting on a sure thing," I said.

Caesar pointed to him. "You be knowing something we don't?"

Milo held his hands in the air. "Would I be tricking

you? I ain't nothing but a team-driving, hardworking black man."

"If I win," I said, "I want your turn sitting up front."

Milo shook his head. "You be driving a hard bargain, Jacob." He bet Kentucky Bob for his bed, Caesar for his second cup of cider, and Seth for a good word with Hannah, the healer. Seth refused, and they left the table to walk outside.

"Milo," I asked, "why were you and Eliza sold?"

"Master lost the farm."

"And how did you get to Kentucky?" I had left them in Virginia.

"Ain't you talked to Eliza yet?"

We really hadn't dared to talk much so far. I shook my head.

"We was carried from Virginy to Kentucky to work. But the master's wife and two sons died with typhoid fever, and he couldn't manage the farm no more. He needed the money from selling us."

I nodded. "And how're you going to get Honorable to take off his gloves?"

At that point Solomon, who had eaten with Chloe and the women, came up to me grunting. I hated to leave Milo, but at least Solomon didn't mess in his pants anymore.

For years the women had changed his pants, but one old auntie had said, "Ridiculous." In one week she trained Solomon to grunt when he needed the outhouse. And if he knew where it was, he could go by himself.

When I returned from the back, the front door to the split-log inn was open. Everyone was outside. Had I missed something because of Solomon? That thought made me so angry, I gave him a shake and ran out dragging him.

This inn was in the woods off a highway. In the starry night sky the moon was egg shaped, and clouds tugged at its light. Why were the travelers outside?

4

Someone had shouted about shooting stars, and they were all outside, even Honorable Mister. He seemed excited. For several moments I stared. Then I saw two stars seem to fall toward the earth, then end in a blaze of light.

I tried to lift Solomon's chin, but I don't think he noticed the stars. I saw five. Others had seen more.

I loved standing there with Mama and the others, just gazing at the heavens. I squeezed Solomon's hand, and he tugged on mine. He was looking at the ground, though. The other travelers returned to the inn, but the ten of us lingered under the spell of starlight and moonglow.

Honorable flipped back his frock coat, then pulled it closed again in the cold air. He was still young, but he looked less ridiculous now that his stovepipe hat fit him.

Eliza had asked for needles and threads for sewing. The new master sent us to a store by ourselves to purchase sewing supplies. She had stitched a thick band around the inner rim of his stovepipe hat.

Now Honorable Mister looked at us and said, "You know I'm a rich man, not because of California, but because of Colorado. My partner and me struck gold almost two years ago.

"Now," he said, "I ain't told you. Or have I? Men and women of labor, tomorrow we begin to buy stagecoaches and supplies to set off for California. No prairie schooner with slow oxen for us. We're traveling in style."

California sounded good to me, but wasn't it late in the year to go that far? What about cold, snow, ice?

"Now, again," Honorable said, "you men and women know my name. But I reckon I don't know yours. And to make it simple"—here he smiled like a sunflower—"I'm calling all you men Clarence." He nodded to us. "And all you women Jane." He bowed toward the women. "My wife is a few hours' ride from here, and her name is Jane. And, of course, I am the Honorable Mister Clarence Higginboom."

I saw the sneer on Kentucky Bob's face. He seemed to hate this master, but I noticed he hadn't run away yet.

Was our owner too lazy to learn our names? I didn't want to answer to the name of Clarence.

My name was Jacob Israel Christmas and I thought I was thirteen. My mama couldn't remember the year for sure, but she couldn't forget the day I was born. She had been hemming the mistress's ballroom gown on Christmas morning when she went into birthing pains and delivered me. She had named me Jacob Israel; later I named myself Christmas.

As we stood outside a man rode up to the inn. He called, "Higgins, ain't that you?"

"Sure is, Tom," Honorable said. "I been looking for you." It was dark outside, but I could swear he turned red. He didn't take a liking to being called Higgins around us.

"And how's Zeke?" the man asked. As the innkeeper's boy took his horse, the man slapped Honorable Mister on the back.

"Zeke's not doing too well." We slaves stood aside for them.

"What happened?" the man asked.

"He drowned in a river."

"I hear them Colorado rivers are deep," said the man. They both laughed.

Drowned? I thought. A couple of weeks ago Honorable told Sam that his partner had died falling off a cliff. And why was he laughing? As we walked into the inn, Kentucky Bob shook his head. I heard him say, "Dang fool." Chloe frowned.

I felt terrible. Were we owned by a murderer, after all? A killer so dumb he couldn't even remember his falsehoods?

He had bought my loyalty with my mama and my friends, with warm clothes, two big meals a day, riding in a stagecoach, and sleeping in inns. Even in the years in

Boston, I had never been this comfortable. Now I wondered if I could trust the Honorable Mister.

"How're the Knights of the Golden Circle?" the man asked in a lower voice. They went in together, but I also heard the words "Stephen Douglas."

Mr. Stephen Douglas was one of the Democrats running against Mr. Abraham Lincoln. He made the Kansas-Nebraska Act so that any new state could decide whether to adopt slavery. Before then only Southern states below a certain line could choose slavery. I wanted to talk, but Chloe went upstairs with the women.

For a moment I held my head. What should I do?

Milo caught my elbow and whispered, "God gave us two ends to use: one to think with and one to sit with. It be up to us which one we choose. Heads, we win. Tails, we lose." He winked, but what did he mean?

Feeling restless, I took Solomon outside for a walk in the moonlight. He liked to be with me. As we strolled the country lane my head was spinning with worry. Should we run away? Was it right to serve a murderer? Was Honorable a murderer, or was he just so young that he couldn't lie straight twice in a row?

Solomon and me returned and sat on a log beside the rough wooden inn. As the moon rose, the inn hugged us in shadows. Solomon began rocking and playing with his fingers. I sat with my chin on my fist.

Before long three men came out of the inn. Our master was one of them. "What's the plan?" he asked in a low voice.

I leaned back, but they couldn't see us anyway.

"You buying a stagecoach, right?"

"Yes, sure. Three of them."

"After you cross the Missouri River—"

"How do I cross?"

"At St. Joseph. You board a ferry with all your equipment. How did you get there the last time?"

Honorable said, "Butterfield Route, through Texas, Arizona."

"Well, this time you'll head northwest in Kansas and over the prairie. You'll go west along the Platte River in Nebraska. About then you'll meet a black stagecoach with a short Irish driver who wears a green scarf, summer and winter."

"Ain't it late to travel the passes?"

We slaves had been talking about that. Milo tried to bet as to whether we'd freeze to death or not, but Eliza told Milo he made bad luck. Polly said it could take four months to travel to California in good weather, and Hannah said it could take fifty or sixty days just to reach Salt Lake City. One of their masters had returned from the 1849 gold rush in California.

"Returned without a cent," Hannah had said.

Now I was pleased to hear that Honorable Mister was aware of the danger. Leaving in late October for

California wasn't wise, it was "dang foolish," as Kentucky Bob would say. I listened.

"You're there to rob money off the black stagecoach," one of the men said.

"Stealing that cash coming east will stop the Pony Express from carrying election news to California," said the other man. "Word of who won will confuse the West."

"We need to hold the news until after the vote for secession," the first man said.

I held my head. California and secession? There were rumors everywhere about the South seceding. Would California leave the Union along with the South? I clenched my fist.

An old lady in Boston had told me this was the best country in the world. And she was a former slave. She said one day people would realize that colored people and white people, we were all created equal. We all had rights.

Our United States Constitution gave hope to slaves, but California wanted to secede? Their gold filled our United States Treasury and made us a rich nation. Everyone knew that. We couldn't lose California. I kept listening.

Honorable Mister said, "You know I'm for a separate Republic of the Pacific."

"First you help us secede. And then, who knows? Maybe they'll be so grateful, they'll make you 'el presi-

dente' of the Republic of the Pacific." Laughing, the man patted Honorable on the head as if our master were a child.

With that, the three walked away talking. I felt chilled to the spine. What could I do? Solomon, who had been listening, sat upright with lips parted. Taking his hand, I stood up slowly, and we slid in shadows around the inn. I had to find out more about their plans, so I guided Solomon around buckets, logs split for burning, and a broken harness.

I wouldn't let Solomon go into the moonlight. I needed to learn everything I could about robbing that stagecoach. Once Solomon wiggled his fingers in the light, but I caught them.

When we reached the men, I realized we were in danger. They stood talking next to a covered well. A maid dumping something walked past us, and saw us, but she didn't give us away. I pressed Solomon against the split-log inn, and I listened.

". . . boys have to be paid. It's already bankrupt, that Pony Express. Without wages, the riders will stop."

So that was it.

"And I rob the stagecoach to stop their pay," said Honorable.

I felt like adding: And I, Jacob Israel Christmas, stop you!

5

I was the only one who knew that our Honorable Mister was not very honorable. No more doubt. To think that I had worried about him sleeping in the room with slaves like Kentucky Bob. Now I worried about us slaves sleeping in the room with him. Murderer. Liar. Thief.

I had to stop Honorable from that robbery. I had no idea how, but I knew I must.

I wondered how much Solomon understood. As we washed for the night, he seemed to be thinking. He had never spoken, so he wouldn't tell.

That night after supper I slid into a seat next to Eliza.

"I thought I'd never see you again, Mama," I said in a whisper. Honorable and the others were gone upstairs. It had taken so long to get to talk in private.

We sat at one of ten trestle tables in the corner of the inn's dining room. Three walls were pinewood, but a fire hissed in a wall-of-stone fireplace. The room smelled of hickory smoke. As Mama squeezed my hand, fire danced beside us.

"Morning and evening I prayed to God for you. And now we're together. But, Jacob Israel, I worry about this young master."

"Eliza," I said, "I be here to take care of you." I wouldn't tell her about those robbery plans. She worried enough as it was.

"This foolish master be dangerous for you, Jacob Israel. Hannah searched his bags, and he ain't got nor whip nor gun. How's he think he'll keep his slaves?"

I asked, "If he was beating us, would you feel better?"

"They'll all be running soon," she said, shaking her head. Mama was only thirty, but suffering made her look fifty. Before I was born, an overseer shot my daddy for visiting her. I think that changed her life.

"Running? Maybe," I said. "Kentucky Bob keeps talking. Seth, too, but they ain't gone yet."

"Well, Jacob Israel, when you see the chance to run, go. Don't you wait to say no good-byes."

"Mama, I ran before, Caesar and me. Bounty hunters brought us back. We were whipped and left at the post for a day and a night without water. They locked us in a shed with nothing to eat or drink. If the slaves hadn't slipped in the window with water, I would have died."

"Jacob Israel," Eliza said, clutching my arm, "I knew pain in my heart for you. My prayers must have saved you." She wiped at a tear.

"If Mr. Abraham Lincoln gets elected president, they

say he'll stop slavery," I told her. "He said the Union can't live half slave and half free. Mama, maybe we'll be freed."

"Is that so? Well now, I'll be praying for that Mr. Lincoln." Eliza was so strong on prayer, I felt much better.

Early the next morning I awoke hearing Honorable patting his blankets. In the faint light I saw him dump his stovepipe hat. Kentucky Bob sat up; he always got a bed to himself. Solomon and I were by Caesar's bed on the floor.

"Clarence?" our master said in a low voice.

No one answered. Seth sat up. He and Milo shared a bed. Honorable Mister, of course, was in a bed all by himself.

"Clarence," he said again, "where are my gloves?"

In the glimmer of early morning I saw Milo smile and lean on one elbow. Had he taken the gloves to win his bet? I sat up, hugged my knees, and got ready for something interesting. Beside me, Solomon was awake and listening.

When I turned to check on him, he handed me the gloves. Oh no! Now I was in trouble. How would I return them?

In the dark I crawled to Caesar and pressed the gloves into his hand, then crawled back. It was a mean thing to do. He shook a fist at me and tossed the gloves to Seth. When Seth saw them, he jumped as if a snake had bitten him. He pushed them toward Milo.

Milo calmly picked them up and slid off the bed.

Walking to Honorable's bed, he said, "Here they be. Dropped on the floor, sir."

"Thank you, Clarence."

Now we would know whether any fingers were missing. As I dressed in the dark I grinned over our bet, but I couldn't remember which side I had taken. After all, it was just for fun.

For breakfast we drank hot cider and ate corn muffins with slabs of ham, sunny-side up eggs on a platter—all we wanted—and gooseberry jam. When Honorable finished and left the dining room, we all jumped up and gathered around Milo.

"Who wants to take bets on California?" he said.

Kentucky Bob slapped his back. "You know what we want. Settle on his fingers first."

I laughed. Milo was always fooling folks.

He looked sheepish. "I reckon I didn't see at all. I held his gloves out, but when he didn't reach for them, I had to lay them down. He's lost fingers all right."

That morning after only four hours by coach, we reached an inn where the Honorable Mister introduced us to his wife. Now we understood why she hadn't traveled with him.

Young Mistress Jane Higginboom was as short as me, with blue eyes, a head full of yellow, sausage-shaped curls, and a high voice. She was also in the family way.

Would our owner carry her on rough, rutted roads in

the cold of winter two thousand miles to California? I just knew that Milo was figuring the odds of her and the baby making it. Hannah, nurse healer and midwife, closed her eyes and shook her head.

Seth's face looked pained; he crossed his arms. The women said he was still grieving his wife and child who died birthing. I knew he didn't want this mistress to lose her baby.

Honorable's wife looked us over, and Solomon began to rock. Before I could catch his hands, he held his fingers to his face.

Mistress Jane grabbed her neck and gave a screech. Her eyes were bulged, her face pale. "Clarence," she called, "why is that boy here? You didn't pay money for that sick-in-the-head boy, did you?"

Honorable Mister glanced at Solomon. "Never you mind," he said to his wife, hugging her. She leaned into his arms and seemed to recover. Kentucky Bob pulled Solomon out of sight behind him and Caesar.

"You ain't used to buying slaves, Clarence. I reckon you did good." She frowned at us. "I ain't used to them neither."

"You have these women of labor to serve you, lovely lady," said her husband with a bow. He liked bowing.

Eliza, Hannah, Polly, and Chloe bowed.

"So, Clarence," said Mistress Jane, "what're we doing now?"

"Never you mind your pretty little head," he said. "These Janes here will tend to you while I take the men to buy supplies."

Eliza rolled her eyes. Healing Hannah shook her head at Milo. It seemed she liked him even without Seth's approval. Hannah and Polly, the cook, wearing that red head wrap, walked into the inn with the new mistress.

After squeezing Eliza's hand and nodding in reply to her look of warning, I followed the men with Solomon. Eliza was so afraid that I'd be harmed somehow.

At the coach store Solomon and I wandered, looking. When something interested him, he could be aware. Whoever named him didn't know what he would be like. King Solomon was wise, but my Solomon was neither wise nor foolish. Most of the time he was "somewhere else," but he did like those coaches.

The Concord coaches had been manufactured in Connecticut and cost over eight hundred dollars each. Like the stagecoaches we had ridden, they carried nine passengers. However, after explaining all that, the salesman warned Honorable:

"We outfit families for the Oregon Trail all the time. Now may I suggest this Kansas-Nebraska ox wagon with wheels high enough to ford a swollen river?"

"No, no."

"Or this Conestoga wagon made in the Conestoga valley of Lancaster County, Pennsylvania? Great on the trails and won't jar apart on rough roads."

What was he talking about? Ford rivers? Jar apart? And was our master buying the wrong kind? I had a purpose now, so I couldn't run, but I was concerned. As Solomon played with his fingers I stooped to look under those wagons.

"No wagons, I'm a rich man," said Honorable. "And this time I'll be traveling in comfort. I've got twenty of the best slaves to keep my coaches in good condition."

What a liar. He had ten slaves and no tools.

"How many coaches do you require? Are your slaves walking behind the coach?"

"No, no, we're all riding. Two coaches would be fine, but I'll take three because I'm a rich man." Honorable tilted his stovepipe hat.

I remembered that he had told those men he would have three coaches.

"Well," said the salesman, leading us back to the Concord coaches, "these are our finest."

I stooped to look under the coaches, and Solomon knelt. There were bolts under the coach and a space between floorboards and bottom. I supposed it could be used for storage.

Solomon bumped me. I wondered if he needed to go to an outhouse, but head down, he rocked on his knees and pointed with his elbow. Finally I noticed something. No fifth wheel under two of the three coaches. I looked around; the grown-up slaves had wandered away. I had to tell our master myself.

Honorable had begun to pay. Just as he was handed something to sign, I coughed and beckoned. I was grateful when he left the salesman and walked over to me.

"Honorable Mister Higginboom," I whispered, "Solomon noticed that there's no fifth wheel under two of your coaches."

He held a hand by his face and asked: "If it rolls on four wheels, why do I need a fifth wheel, Clarence?"

"Because wheels break, sir," I said. "All the wagons and coaches carry a spare wheel." Didn't he know that? Even in cities, wheels broke. What was wrong with this master?

"Good, good, Clarence." Without checking under the coaches for himself, he strode over to the waiting clerk. "Why're you cheating me? There's no fifth wheel!"

"Oh, oh," the man said. His eyes shot poisoned arrows at me. We waited while fifth wheels were found and attached under the two coaches.

Solomon sat under one of the coaches playing with his fingers. I didn't think he'd leave, so I walked outside.

Caesar was down the block and waved for me to come. Around the corner he showed me a storefront window. Three boys in red shirts and blue pants stood holding Bibles. A bearded man led them in a pledge.

"I do hereby swear, before the great and living God, that during my engagement, and while I am an employee of Russell, Majors, and Waddell, I will under no circumstances use profane language; that I will drink no intoxicating liquors; that I will not quarrel or fight with any other employee of the firm; and that in every respect I will conduct myself honestly, be faithful to my duties, and so direct all my acts as to win the confidence of my employers. So help me God."

The boys fit the Bibles into their shirts.

Caesar whispered, "Pony Express riders."

"And, men," said the man with brown whiskers, "you'll be paid promptly. Any day now I expect a government contract from Congress. Until the telegraph catches up, we're the riders of the night, the couriers of the day. Since April third this year ours has been the honor of crossing our nation to deliver mail. You're joining a noble troop of riders."

He went on: "Money is kept at both ends of the mail delivery for your weekly wages. Twenty-five dollars."

Caesar looked bug-eyed. People worked hard for three or maybe five dollars a week. And these Pony Express riders made twenty-five dollars?

The bearded man lowered his voice: "By telegraph sent from Washington, we'll hear who's elected president of these United States. You Pony Express riders will be honored to carry that news over the prairie, across our great American desert, and through mountain passes. The fate of our nation for the next four years depends on the election news reaching California."

He paused and said, "Look at those pitiful creatures outside the window."

He meant me and Caesar. The riders turned to stare at us.

"Will our nation continue treating people worse than we treat animals? Will that system of slavery spread to the great western states?"

As their swearing-in ended I trembled.

These were new riders. I would make sure their pay arrived in the East. So much depended on the Pony Express traveling to California. I said to myself: Yes, I must stop that robbery. I hoped I could.

6

It was October by the time we reached St. Joseph, Missouri. We stayed at a luxury hotel called Patee House. Standing around on the deep carpet were Pony Express riders in their blue-fringed pants. As Honorable Mister arranged for our rooms at a handsome wooden counter, I walked with Solomon among the red-shirted riders. We overheard their talk:

"Pay not there. I don't wanna ride."

"They say Russell is bankrupt."

"But he just told us 'bout the contract."

"Contract from Washington never coming."

Chloe walked over to stand beside us. A dozen upholstered chairs and settees faced off in cozy circles. We slaves stood in a corner. I hadn't told Chloe about the stagecoach robbery plans yet.

She whispered, "Never mind the Pony Express. Mr. Abraham Lincoln will bring us freedom."

"Suppose Mr. Stephen Douglas wins?" I said.

"He'll allow slavery wherever people want it. That

would be terrible. These last weeks I almost feel free, you know? But I could be sold again. And to a master who would make me suffer."

We watched as a family arrived with a slave. Although he was young, he walked in a shuffle, his head bowed. The owner gave orders in a loud voice, and the slave said, "Yes, suh, Marster."

I felt horrible. Had I been like that only a few weeks ago? With a frown, Kentucky Bob walked out the hotel door and slammed it. It seemed seeing that slave made him angry too. We ten slaves were no longer shuffling with bowed heads. Honorable let us look him in the eye—something most masters wouldn't allow.

That slave and others around town had me wondering. When would the bad times return? I didn't say anything; I listened to Chloe.

"I'd give my life to breathe as a free girl for a few minutes," she said with a sigh. Would she and Seth run soon?

Milo walked over. "We be going for supplies and to buy horses, Jacob. Want to come?" Four slave men and Honorable stood by the hotel door.

As a joke I said, "Buy an extra horse for me to ride."

Honorable nodded. "Good plan, Clarence boy," he called. "I'll want to ride outside the coach sometimes myself. We'll get two extra horses."

Did he mean that? Would he buy a horse for me? "Thank you, Honorable Mister Higginboom," I said, bowing. I thought, "honorable" or "dishonorable"?

When they walked out, I turned to Chloe. "I have to tell you something." With Solomon between us, we walked through the dining rooms and kitchen of the long hotel. I told her everything Solomon and I had heard about Honorable robbing the black stagecoach and about California leaving the Union.

Chloe shrugged. "California be a long, long ways from Washington City. Why would anyone worry about whether California secedes with the South? Or becomes a republic?"

I shook my head. "Don't you know about the United States?" I told her about our Constitution and our Bill of Rights.

"But, Jacob, why California?"

"Chloe," I said, "California has gold. All over the world you can buy things with gold. If the North has gold, they can buy guns to fight a war. If the South has gold, they can buy guns. If it comes down to a war over slavery and the Union, the side with the gold wins."

"Gold," she said, "be yellow metal."

"You know about the Golden Rule?" I asked.

"Sure. 'Do unto others as you would have them do unto you.'"

"Wrong."

"Wrong? What'd you mean, wrong?" Chloe put her hands on her hips and frowned.

"The Golden Rule," I said, "is this: Them with the gold rule." She grinned.

"Chloe, we have to save California for the Union."

"Jacob," she said, "we have to save California for freedom. You be saying California's gold might pay for a war and buy our liberty for Mr. Lincoln. What can we do?"

"Make sure our master doesn't steal the money on that black stagecoach. Do everything we can to keep the Pony Express moving across the country. We have to listen and be ready." When I said that, I noticed that Solomon nodded.

That night in the hotel parlor I overheard that a man named Mr. Edward Creighton had left the hotel to map the route for telegraph poles. Getting news from the East to the West by wires would be easy. I suppose I hadn't hidden my expression of wonder because a man called, "Boy, I see you're interested in the telegraph. We're short of workers. Could you help us with the poles and wire across the river in Kansas?"

This would be a chance to do something. No matter how small. Solomon and I together. If we only helped with one pole or one wire, we would do it.

"If our master, Honorable Mister Clarence Higginboom, allows," I told the man.

"I'll go see him."

As a result, all of us but Milo were hired out to the

telegraph company. It was better than standing around that hotel watching families with slaves.

St. Joseph was crowded with people outfitting themselves for winter in the West. Flour, sugar, coffee, clothing, boots, oxen, saddles, mules, horses, wagons. Everything was for sale. Seemed people were buying supplies to last all year. Like a hive of bees in flight, anxious families swarmed the streets.

Colorful Pony Express boys and rough-looking telegraph men added even more excitement. These were times of long-distance advancement.

Chloe stayed with the women, and Milo helped Honorable choose horses. Solomon and me went with the other men to work on the transcontinental telegraph system.

The next morning five of us rode in a bouncing wagon all the way down to the Missouri River. Telegraph wagons and horses rolled onto the ferry. Solomon stayed in the wagon with Caesar and Seth, but I stood up front in the ferryboat looking at the water. The river reflected blue sky and clouds, and the breeze made me turn up my collar.

Kentucky Bob stood by me and said, "This here is work for pay. I could just run away and work for these men." I shook my head. We both knew he would be put in jail as an escaped slave. I turned to him. I probably shouldn't have asked, but I did.

"Why do you look angry all the time?"

His scar grew red. Over the last few days I had grown to like Kentucky Bob. As the ferry moved, his long brown hair blew in breezes. His bushy eyebrows almost joined when he frowned. He may have been violent, but he respected the women, never cussing near them. Also, he looked out for Solomon, making sure he was served food.

"Well," he said, "I took it hard when my father sold me." I looked at him. What did he mean? But I knew.

"Master was my father, and he raised me with my mama in a cabin in Maryland. Then when I was sixteen and talked back, he sold me. My sweet mama died two days later. From grief." He groaned and touched his scar.

"The man what cut my face? Was my own father, with a cane knife from the field. Meanest man I ever knew."

So all folks had their story. There was something else I needed to know. "Why did you walk over to join us at the auction?"

"Jacob," he said, "I saw you and them women holding Solomon's hands. And somehow I felt y'all be such dang fools, y'all needed me."

I laughed. Kentucky Bob wasn't all bad. When the ferry landed, I walked beside him to join Solomon in the wagon. Half a mile out in the Kansas grassland we stopped.

A wagon load of poles had been dropped off, and

telegraph men with instruments called transits were sur-
veying the land. Boys younger than me held sticks painted
with lines. They said the surveyors made sure the telegraph
poles and wires traveled straight.

We were put to work digging holes five feet deep, for
posts twelve inches in diameter. Men dug with narrow,
long-handle spades, and Solomon and I hauled away the
buckets of dirt. For weeks I hadn't done any labor, and at
first I was almost panting.

Seth had enough breath to dig and sing. At the Patee
House he had learned "Little Old Sod Shanty" about
claiming land in the West. Would slaves ever be free to
homestead?

Seth sang:

"I'm looking rather seedy now while holding down my claim,
And my vittles are not always of the best.
And the mice play shyly 'round me as I nestle down to rest
In my little old sod shanty on the plain.

Oh, the hinges are of leather and the windows have no glass,
The boards, they let the howling blizzard in,
You can see the hungry coyote as he sneaks up through the grass,
To my little old sod shanty on the plain.

I rather like the novelty of living in this way,
Though my bill of fare ain't always of the best,

But I'm happy as a clam, on the land of Uncle Sam,
In my little old sod shanty in the West."

After singing a while with Seth, the work felt good. For lunch they fed us big bowls of white beans and fresh bread with coffee. The weather was blowing cold, and the coffee was steaming hot. I drank it bitter, with grounds in the bottom of the cup.

While I watched, men raised telegraph poles coated with creosote and called Black Jacks. Solomon and I searched for stones to fill a basket we dragged along the ground. After the Black Jacks were set in holes, we helped fill the holes with stones.

"Filling in with stones keeps the poles erect better than soft dirt," a man told us.

As we dumped stones I overheard someone say, "Lincoln'll just bring war. You read his House Divided speech about a half-slave and half-free country not surviving. Them Fire Eaters in the South will never give up their slaves. Lincoln's a fool."

Another man said, "It's not moral to keep a man a slave. Slaves should earn their freedom after twenty years or so. Did you read *Uncle Tom's Cabin?*"

"I saw the play. Very sad. But the time ain't right to free slaves."

As I dumped more stones I said, "We can't wait. The time ain't never going to be right." Luckily, they didn't hear me.

Men rolled huge wooden spools of wire that had been covered with something called gutta-percha. Glass insulators held the wires on the poles.

"Solomon," I said, "words travel along those wires."

He dumped the last stone and turned, but I felt a sense of awe. We were living in an exciting age. Words could actually be taken off a wire charged by an electric battery. I shook my head in amazement.

"Know how we dig when the earth's frozen?" a man asked me. As grasses bent in breezes he stood to rest.

"No, sir."

"We scoop out a bowl, dump a cask of quicklime in it, and pour water. That'll thaw it down to six feet, but Lord help the man quicklime splashes on."

He showed me scars burned on his arms and face. He said, "Most of them linemen got them same scars. Some lose fingers."

Fingers! Had Honorable lost a finger or two as a lineman?

The man pointed. "There's a brass pounder. Ain't he a dandy?"

The brass pounder looked dressed for an evening tea. He wore a blue serge suit and a bowler hat with a high crown. I looked at my new gray suit and brushed off dust. That young man had a green brocade vest with a gold watch chain. In Boston I had heard about brass pounders.

They worked the telegraph keys, writing down and passing along as many as four messages at a time. Like the Pony Express riders, they earned good wages. All these new jobs men and boys could work filled me with wonder. If only I were free.

I wondered if Kentucky Bob could succeed if he ran away. Those Fugitive Slave Laws were upheld in Missouri and Kansas.

Later that first day when Solomon and I were hauling stones, I heard a shout from one of the men: "Here he comes!"

I turned to see what he was talking about. Far away in the prairie I saw a figure riding toward us. The blue and red I knew. This was a Pony Express boy carrying mail. At last I would see one in action.

Catching Solomon by the sleeve, I pulled him over to Milo, who leaned on his shovel. "Riding a California mustang," said Milo. "Wild horses. Meaner than rattlesnakes, swifter than eagles."

I not only saw puffs of dust and grass in the air, but under my feet I felt the thuds of horse hooves. What a thrill to see someone galloping that fast! And to know that the Pony Express was carrying mail west to California was even more fascinating. That rider was tying our nation together.

The Pony Express rider seemed not much older than

me. As he raced nearer he pulled out a bugle and blew three blasts. My skin tingled and my scalp crawled. I held Solomon's hand, and how he stared! He wasn't playing with his fingers or rocking; he seemed thrilled.

The rider wore his red shirt open at the neck over winter underwear, and his blue pants with fringe on the sides waved in the breeze. His face was freckled, his neck sunburned red, and his legs short.

I noticed the square leather blanket he was sitting on. It fit snugly over the horn of the saddle on the mustang. That was where the mail was kept.

"What's it called?" I asked in a whisper as I pointed.

Beside us someone said, "That's called a mochila." The rider passed us, stirring up a whirlwind.

At each corner of the leather blanket there was a pouch that read MAIL. The four mailbags had padlocks on them.

"Who has the keys?" I asked.

"Keys are kept in St. Joseph, Missouri; in Salt Lake City, Utah; and in Sacramento, California," a man told me.

I wondered if any black boys got a chance to ride the Pony Express. This was the mail delivery I had read about in the newspapers. I smiled at Solomon, but he didn't smile back.

Every day after that I looked for the Pony Express rider.

For about five days we worked hauling stones and filling

holes for telegraph poles. Chloe was angry that she couldn't come, but I told her she had to listen in the hotel.

One morning she told me: "Jacob Israel, there's a big plot I heard about. The Pony Express rider brought news of it to telegraph to President Buchanan. It's all about California and the South. They're preparing for war all right."

7

"What did you hear?" I asked Chloe that morning at the hotel. Honorable hadn't hired us out anymore. Since they laid about five miles of telegraph wire a day, the work was getting to be farther and farther away. We had been returning too late.

She pointed to a rider in the parlor. "He be the one telling the others."

The Pony Express boy smiled at Chloe and said, "You mean about the Secretary of War?"

She nodded, and the rider strutted over to where we stood in a corner of the plush parlor. Slaves and freemen mingled here. Everyone was so excited about leaving or returning from the West, they didn't worry about a boy's position in life.

Still, as a slave, I felt honored to have this young man talk with us. Of course, Chloe was pretty and attracted boys. I hated the way men looked at her. I wanted to tell them, She's mine.

That morning she wore her short black hair in five

cornrows with the braids tucked in at the neck.

As the rider told his story, he grinned at her.

"I saw a shipment of two cannons, a box of rifles, and boxes of ammunition at the dock in San Francisco," he said. "As I walked by I heard a man say they were getting shipments from Springfield, Massachusetts, thanks to Mr. John B. Floyd.

"'Which John B. Floyd?'" the other man asked.

"'Why, President Buchanan's Secretary of War,'" the first man answered.

"I brought back word with the mail delivery," the rider said. "They telegraphed it from here to Washington. Sure enough, a member of the president's cabinet was in a conspiracy against the Union. He had been supplying weapons to some Southern states, too. But President Buchanan'll stop him."

The rider winked at me. "The Pony Express saved the day," he said.

I thought: And I'll save the Pony Express!

"My name be Jacob Israel Christmas," I said, offering to shake hands; some white boys wouldn't shake a slave's hand, but this rider had a strong, friendly grip.

"Glad to make your acquaintance," he said. "My name is Boston Ben Smith. Let me introduce you to some of the others."

Boston Ben? Was he really from Boston? I had lived there.

He waved for me to leave Chloe and walk over. I wanted to meet those boys with their exciting jobs, but I had left Chloe all day for five days.

"My friend needs to know about the Pony Express," I said. The riders were talking men-talk. Nevertheless, I decided to take Chloe over. They would just have to talk around a girl for a change.

"Sure enough," said Boston Ben, "bring him along." He glanced around for another slave boy, but I led Chloe over.

The group laughed as we walked near. "If the Paiutes and Shoshones don't get you, the road agents will," a rider said.

"No wonder they advertised for orphans as riders," another rider said. They all laughed again, and I noticed that no one was drinking ale. But then again, they had taken that pledge.

How I admired them! I promised myself to tell Chloe about their swearing-in ceremony. I liked sharing news with her.

"They give us a rifle, but for the Indians, I carry blankets." The rider shoved his hands in his pockets.

"I carry cornmeal," a red-haired rider said. "The Shoshones are often hungry. If you offer corn for a night's meal, you win a friend who'll rescue you if you're sick and protect you against road agents."

"Who're road agents?" I asked.

"Outlaws," they all said together.

"This is Jacob," said Boston Ben.

"And Chloe," I added. They all shook hands with us and told us their exciting names: Rusty Jack, Nick, Dandy Dan, Kansas Gordon, and Boston Ben. They stood boldly in the center of the parlor.

"Road agents are outlaws, white men out to steal," said Dandy Dan. "I'd rather meet an Indian brave than a road agent any day."

"But your mail pouches are padlocked," I said.

"If a road agent thinks there's gold or important mail, he'll shoot off the locks or cut open the pouches. They're only leather."

The other riders nodded and shifted feet on the thick carpet.

"Once I had to carry silver as well as mail," one rider said. "And the mochila pouches swung low. So I covered them with an old mochila and stuffed the false mail pouches with cut newspaper and rocks. Sure enough, down a hillside came this white man with a mustache dragging the ground."

They all laughed and barely moved aside for a family.

"He demanded my mail pouches. My horse was fresh, and his was old. So I swung the fake mochila off, leaped into the saddle, and rode off. By the time he discovered his newspaper and rocks, I was long gone."

Everyone laughed again.

"The worst time is when the relay station is empty."

"Or burned out by Indians."

"Or the mustangs have been stolen."

Boston Ben said, "Nothing worse than reaching a home station and finding the rider can't relieve you."

"Right," said Nick. "When you had that arrow in your shoulder, I had to ride all day."

"I could have ridden," Boston Ben said, wincing as he patted his left shoulder. "The stationmaster insisted on removing the arrow and pouring in whiskey."

Beside me, Chloe drew her breath sharply.

"Whiskey?" said Rusty Jack. He leaned against a dark blue chair. "That's a humbug way to earn a drink."

The riders all chuckled at that.

Rusty Jack pulled up his sleeve. "Lucky day when the bullet went through flesh but didn't hit bone. I outrode the outlaw."

Chloe said softly, "Y'all be so brave."

"I began riding this spring in April. This winter'll be our test. And sometimes we ride without pay," said Nick. "You know what they call the Central Overland California and Pike's Peak Express Company these days?"

That was the official name of the Pony Express.

"Clean Out of Cash and Poor Pay Express Company," he said. How they roared at that!

Kansas Gordon said, "I don't care what they promise. If they don't pay, I don't ride." He folded his arms.

I glanced at Chloe. That's why we had to save their wages.

"We're a page in history," said Boston Ben softly. "The telegraph will take our place soon. But in ten days instead of fifty, we tie this nation together, Atlantic to Pacific." He seemed dedicated, and I liked that.

Rusty Jack nodded his long red hair. "You heard the story of the United States senator elected from California? By the time he reached Washington, his term of office was over."

Chloe and I laughed along with the boys. Solomon came over, and with a reluctant wave, we walked away. He bumped my shoulder twice. I tried to lift his chin to peek at his face, but he wouldn't look at me.

"Something's happening," I told Chloe.

"Should we follow him?" she asked.

Solomon walked ahead, then glanced back. Chloe ran for her shawl, I donned my jacket, and we followed him through the hotel.

Out back the men were packing our three coaches with pots, pans, picks, rope, harnesses, blankets, and other supplies. When he saw me, Milo waved in the air.

"He bought twenty head of horses," he said. "For two days I tried to sell him on mules or oxen, but he wanted stagecoach harness horses not meant for western trails." Milo shook his head.

I felt worried. Honorable wasn't quite a simpleton, but

he wasn't a wise person, either. Those robbery men seemed to be using him, and now, according to Milo, he hadn't followed good judgment.

"I'm still choosing the teams," Milo said. "Some horses won't lead, while others want to lead. Some won't run next to another horse but have to be in back. Others seem to like to run beside a certain horse. I've had three days to do a month's work."

Again Solomon bumped me and bent down. "Stand there," I told Chloe, and I crawled under a coach with Solomon. He put his head down. I knew he was trying to say something important. Suppose we had accepted the coaches without spare wheels?

Months ago Solomon had bumped me the night on the plantation when Caesar and I discovered that Sarah had taken her seven children and had driven off in our former master's buggy. All the slaves were worried. With no help, no food, no plans, Sarah just rode off. Solomon kept bumping me that night.

When I had asked, "What can I do?" he put his head down.

Caesar had said, "What you reckon we could do to give her a chance of escaping with them children? She be crazy, you know."

Solomon had bumped me again. "Let's figure," I'd said. "What would make Master so angry, he wouldn't think about following her?"

Solomon had looked up. With an elbow, he'd pointed to the distant barn. "He's proud of his tobacco harvest," I'd said. "That be it."

Caesar and I poured kerosene around the storage barn. Its smell on our hands and clothes gave us away, but we set a great fire. Sarah and her seven children might have made it to Canada.

Now this time what did Solomon want me to know? I knew I had to find out what he wanted me to see.

8

As I crouched under the coach looking around, I heard Caesar complain about having to choose the tools to buy. Seth grumbled about following Polly as she planned meals from flour, sugar, oil, coffee, molasses, smoked beef, ham, bacon, dried fruit. Kentucky Bob growled about helping Hannah buy bandages, salves, and ointments. Our master had given them full responsibility, and he had paid the bills.

Honorable was a lucky man to buy us ten slaves. All of us were smart, except for poor Solomon. He didn't help much.

Eliza kept saying, "I be so worried that what we doing be wrong. Ain't never had no master knew less than I did." She sat on a stool sewing horse blankets. At Milo's request she was joining blankets and adding straps to cover the animals at night.

"Sure you did," Milo said, "but them other masters never let on when they be dumb."

Solomon and I sat under the coach listening. Finally I

looked up and saw a box. Wooden boxes hadn't been under the coaches before. Solomon nodded and began to rock. Crawling on hands and knees, I saw that a box had been nailed under each of the three coaches.

Solomon bumped me again, and I turned the latch on one box. It opened. Raising the lid, I touched a burlap bag. I loosened a drawstring and reached inside. For a moment I remembered a sack with a snake inside, and I winced. There was no snake inside this bag; it was full of shiny gold coins that glowed in my hand by sunlight.

For a second Solomon showed his lit-candle smile. Then he crawled out. After closing that box and crawling around to check both of the others, I followed him.

How unbelievable! I felt dizzy. Here I was, a thirteen-year-old boy, used to being told what to do as a slave, and now I knew things I shouldn't. Should I tell someone about the gold? Eliza? Caesar? Milo? I had to make that decision all by myself.

Under our coaches Honorable Mister Clarence Higginboom had sacks of gold coins worth thousands of dollars. Couldn't someone steal his gold? But who would believe that a man hid gold in three unlocked boxes?

Around me, they were still arguing. My Eliza wrung her hands. "I say it ain't wise to go with this young master."

When she saw me crawl out from under a coach, she said, "Jacob Israel, you should run tonight. Living in the woods be safer than crossing the desert with this mad boy." That was strong language for her.

I thought for a moment before I said, "What does it mean to take a chance, because what you could do might make something happen that might turn out to be good?" I didn't tell them what was on my mind.

"That's called a long shot," said Milo with a grin. "And life be full of them." With a straw in the corner of his mouth, he crossed his arms and leaned against a coach.

"Some folks think life be a battle to fight, but I find life be a creek to walk upstream," Seth said, squatting by a wheel.

Polly added: "Life be like a bunch of herbs, some bitter, some sweet, to season a soup." As she sat on a coach stool she hugged her shawl to her chest.

"But," said Big Caesar, waving a finger, "it ain't never all this way or all that way; it's a mix that's always changing. Remember that."

"That be true," said Kentucky Bob, standing away from the rest of us. "So, boy"—and he looked at me—"this be life." For once he didn't look angry.

Everyone was silent.

Chloe smiled at me. "That be reason for hope," she said.

"Bible says, 'In hope we be saved,'" said Eliza. It was the first positive thing I'd heard Mama say. She pulled her shawl around her and bent to her sewing.

"You folks realize," said Milo, grunting as he sat on a basket, "we being treated like workers who got themselves brains, and we don't like it? Here we be responsible for this—"

"Dang fool," interrupted Kentucky Bob, folding his arms.

"Yeah, this dang fool and his wife staying alive and reaching somewhere called California. This be like freedom."

With gold going west under the coaches, I thought.

"And after we get there, he hire him an overseer and whip us at the biggest tree in California," said Kentucky Bob. "I've had white men beat me for my loyalty. I be running."

I held my head. "I feel like life be dancing all around me," I said, "and I be dizzy from the music."

Never had I had to make decisions like these before, and, I suspected, neither had they. I didn't know what I should do about that gold. Should I tell the others? Could I stop that robbery? Would I be able to save California?

"I be running tonight," said Seth. "I can't stand to see a woman and unborn child put to danger, even if she be a white woman. And I'm taking Polly and Hannah and Chloe with me."

"Not me," said Chloe.

"You may be running, but I ain't," said Polly, tightening her red turban.

"Neither me," Hannah said. "I hear it be warm all year long in California. If I run, I run in California."

Chloe blinked twice at me and walked away. Although I didn't want to leave the others, I followed her with Solomon. When we were alone in a shed behind the Patee House, she said, "Now tell me again, Jacob Israel. Let me get it straight."

"Just Jacob. Only Eliza calls me both names."

"The Dishonorable Mister Higginboom . . ."

I laughed.

". . . is going to steal money from a stagecoach going east. That means it'll meet us on the road and pass us. And we're going to stop him from taking it.

"And the cash be wages for Pony Express riders," she continued. "Because without pay, they won't carry the mail to California. And the important news for them to carry be whether Mr. Lincoln gets elected. And if he be president, he'll need gold from California to fight a war. And if the war be won—"

"Wait," I said, holding up my hand. "Yes, his election news may save California for the Union."

"So somebody thinks."

"Uh, yes, somebody thinks," I said.

"And if Mr. Abraham Lincoln be president, he may free us slaves."

"Well, for sure he don't like slavery spreading," I said slowly. "Now you have me confused."

"Well, you ain't alone," said Chloe, strolling away. She turned and dragged her feet walking back. "Jacob, this be a purpose in life. Besides just staying alive, I ain't never had no need, no reason to live before. Lots of orders from masters and Seth, but no real goal of my own. Maybe I like it." She smiled.

I hadn't told her about those shiny coins under our coaches. Each coin was worth hundreds of dollars, and only Solomon and I knew about them. How many Pony Express riders needed wages? Honorable Mister Higginboom's gold was probably enough to pay all of them.

Why should I worry about a stagecoach going east? How would a man like Honorable, without a gun, steal from a stagecoach? Where would our three coaches stay while he stole it? Or was he planning on one of us stealing the Pony Express money?

Everything else for this trip was done by his "men and women of labor," his "Clarences and Janes." Would some of us end up thieves? Not me, I promised myself.

The next morning before light we gathered our change of clothes, blankets, and the rest of the supplies. Outside on the street three shiny brown coaches stood in the dark. How handsome they seemed, even if they weren't practical for the trip. As our master said, we were traveling in comfort.

All ten of us were there. No one had run away after all. Milo ordered Seth, Caesar, and Kentucky Bob to help fit horses into their harnesses. Heavy sacks of grain—oats and bran—filled the floors of the coaches, along with feed bags and blankets for the horses. Milo even had blocks of salt for the horses to lick.

Swinging lanterns lit all the activity. I climbed into a cozy coach beside Chloe, curled up on a grain bag, and dozed off.

Caesar called, "Get out here, Jacob."

"You mean Clarence," I mumbled as I crawled to the doorway and dropped to the ground.

"Here be your horse you asked for. You ride, boy." He held the reins to a dappled gray mare whose nostrils flared at me.

"Pretty girl," I said softly. Her eyes were full of fear; her ears were slicked back. She whinnied and pranced, but I took her reins and stroked her neck.

"What will you name her?" Chloe asked from inside the coach.

"Pretty Girl."

"Your own horse. Can I ride her sometimes?"

I spoke softly. "Do you know how?"

"I used to ride to carry messages, and not sidesaddle either. Aunt Mary said I wasn't a lady no more."

"Come talk to her," I said. When my horse seemed more settled, I led her away from the business of loading up.

"Solomon should pet her too," said Chloe, and she called him from the coach.

Before long all three of us sat on Pretty Girl's back, and she trotted up and down the St. Joseph street. To the east the sky washed lighter and lighter.

"What's holding us up?" Kentucky Bob asked, frowning. His new-moon scar glowed red. I decided that he made a habit of being angry, just as Eliza made a habit of worrying.

After a while Honorable Mister Higginboom, clutching his hat, walked out the front door of the hotel. "Clarences and Janes," he called, "your mistress ain't feeling so good this morning. She'll be out in a few minutes."

Kentucky Bob waited until Honorable returned inside and closed the hotel door before saying, "Dang fool."

"Do you know where the shovel is for the graves?" asked Milo.

"We need two," said Caesar. "I be digging with you."

"There'll be no graves on this travel," Eliza said. "Shame on you men."

"Bigger shame," said Kentucky Bob, "to leave an infant unburied for the wolves."

Hannah, the midwife, moaned. "Lord help me," she said.

Milo opened his mouth, but Eliza pointed to him. "No bets on who'll be living and who'll be dying. That be in the Lord's hands."

"You men just bring me food to cook," Polly called. "I'll keep us alive."

As I sat on my horse I heard Kentucky Bob say, "I

found me two shovels, but the ground might soon be too frozen to dig."

There was a bustle, and Eliza climbed out of a coach. "Haircuts," she called, clicking her scissors. "And you be first, Jacob Israel."

Chloe got her wish before I thought she would. She and Solomon rode Pretty Girl around the city block while I got the first haircut. Afterward my cap sat better on my head. All the men except Kentucky Bob were sheared like lambs under Eliza's scissors.

Finally by wintry sunrise Mistress Jane Higginboom wobbled out on her husband's arm and used a stool to climb into the first coach.

"Rifles," said Seth. "Do we have rifles to hunt food?"

"I don't think we do, Clarence," said our master. "But a gun shop is on the street leading to the ferry."

Now slaves with rifles? Whoever heard of it? Of course, I helped hunt ducks for my last master. I had shot squirrels, too. However, a gun-toting overseer had stood behind me.

At the gun store Honorable bought rifles and ammunition for Milo, Seth, Caesar, and Kentucky Bob. "My rifle be your rifle," Milo told me. He winked at Hannah. They were friends now.

At last we reached the ferryboat, and we were on our way.

9

Gray skies read November as our coaches crossed on the ferry one at a time. With six horses harnessed to it, a coach took up almost all of the ferryboat's deck. Kentucky Bob, Seth, and Caesar drove the three coaches, in that order. Before the ferry took off, Milo visited each team, calming the jittery horses and teaching the men how to handle them. After we crossed the river, we gathered on the other side in Kansas.

Since Honorable rode in the first coach with his wife, his black horse was tied in back. Chloe asked, "Do you think I could ride it?"

I shrugged. She rode Pretty Girl well enough, but our master's horse was a big black gelding with a braided mane. I thought Chloe shouldn't even ask, but sure enough, in a wink she was riding beside me, with Solomon on the saddle behind her.

I felt angry that a girl was riding a bigger horse than I was. And that she carried Solomon; he was my friend. Why was she taking over?

In Kansas the road wasn't much more than wagon-wheel ruts. Milo asked Kentucky Bob to take the lead coach; Kentucky Bob just sat stiffly and leaned forward as he drove along, but he slowly pulled to the front of our line.

In the distance I noticed where the telegraph men were working. The prairie was a sea of gray-green and tan winter grasses with a bare-limb tree here and there. This flat grassland was as wide as eternity. It seemed I could see all the way to forever. Birds flew from one grass head to another, eating the seeds.

When I listened, I heard them bitty birds a-chirping, and I envied how free they were. My spirit rose up and flew with them, then I felt happy inside. Almost peaceful.

Chloe and I rode in silence behind the last coach. She glanced here and there, catching her breath when she saw a rabbit, a chipmunk, or a red-winged blackbird.

Milo rode on the driver's seat with Caesar, who drove the third coach. From there he could watch the teams driven by Seth and Kentucky Bob. Milo leaned out and waved for me to ride alongside. I caught up slowly, Chloe right behind me.

"We need scouts," he said.

"What do scouts do?" asked Chloe.

"Ride up ahead, see where the trail turns, look out for holes and creeks. But don't get too far ahead."

"I'll go too," she said.

"Watch out for Indians and road agents," Milo said with a mischievous grin. Why would he put us in danger? I felt furious. Chloe was pretending to be so brave. Now I had to scout for bad men.

"Outlaws wouldn't be this close to St. Joseph, would they?" I asked.

Caesar looked grim. "They can be anywhere they want to be."

Solomon blinked to awareness. I think he and I were both thinking of that gold under the coaches. I had made a decision: No one needed to know about our master's gold. Solomon and I were holders of his secret.

On the telegraph wagon we had ridden similar trails, but I hadn't been responsible. Now as I rode ahead I felt the weight of twelve travelers and twenty horses on my shoulders.

Right away I pointed. "Could a horse break a leg in a hole like that?" Or a coach break a wheel? I wondered.

Chloe said, "They could swing around there and miss it." She pointed to some tall grass.

I rode over. Another coach had circled the spot. Were there going to be sinkholes that often? Suppose I missed one and a horse broke its leg? Could a beautiful animal need to be shot, just because of me?

I said, "I guess we tell Kentucky Bob."

"Sure," said Chloe.

We looked at each other. I think she and I both

dreaded being responsible for the teams and coaches. Where was Honorable? Why was he leaving everything to us? Again.

After about four hours of tense riding Milo halted the coaches. He ordered Kentucky Bob, Seth, and Caesar to pull off the trail on the river side. When I dismounted, I was so stiff, I could hardly walk.

Mistress Jane climbed down from her coach, walked a few steps, and cried out: "Why are all these burrs and thistles here, Clarence?"

"Why, lovely lady, there ain't much other place we could stop."

"Order these people to clear them away. They're sticking to my skirt and shawl," she said, jerking at her clothes.

"Yes, lovely."

Our master had better sense than to tell us to clear the prairie. Besides, everyone was bustling with new obligations, and most of us seemed grumpy about them. Even the gray sky oozed worry and the shifting clouds seemed nervous.

Solomon wandered through the grass. From time to time he stopped to pick up a rock. He had gathered rocks for the telegraph poles, and now he seemed to have a new pastime. It was better than finger-play.

Milo ordered the men to free the horses from their harnesses for watering. That was work. Chloe and I led our horses, but the riverbank was steep and muddy. She slid down off her horse on her back. When I tried to pull her up, I fell on my knees in the mud. My horse started off. Twice I slipped trying to catch the reins.

Half of the first day had passed, and already I wanted to go back. A stiff breeze chilled me to the bone, especially where I was wet. I wanted to cry, but not in front of Chloe.

"This wind will dry us fast," she said.

I just looked at her. That pleasant little prophecy made me angry. I would have felt better if Chloe had told me I'd catch a fever and die.

Milo and Seth were dry, but Caesar and Kentucky Bob had fallen in the water. Kentucky Bob swore under his breath when he wasn't near any of the women.

Chloe said, "You know what I named my horse?"

When I didn't answer, she said, "Black Midnight."

We all seemed mad as hornets from a broken nest when Milo whistled and pointed. A single oxbow wagon with a bleached-white canvas cover and two black oxen rolled along the trail. Somehow the sight cheered me up. Here were people who had made it coming east.

Stovepipe hat on head, Honorable Mister strutted up to the trail. Five people on the wagon gave us a cheer as they drew near. "Where you from?" called Honorable.

"Salt Lake City," the driver said. "How far to St. Joseph?"

"About four hours," we all called. I wished I were returning to that plush hotel in the city.

"How's the trail?" our master asked.

"Well, some Indians swept down and stole our horses, but they didn't want our oxen. A road agent with a long mustache came along and stole our money, our rings, and our watch. Already there's snow in the Rockies, and we found that the Platte River is almost dry in some places. How far you people traveling?"

"California," said Honorable.

The people on the wagon laughed. Three white men, two white women. A slave woman holding a white child looked out of the wagon. Seven people altogether.

"Good luck," they called, and rolled on.

As I stood staring after them I envied them, and I bet I wasn't alone. What about that outlaw? And Indians stealing horses? We were at the mercy of our horses; without them, we couldn't move. Milo looked serious, and I wondered if he was betting odds.

The men returned the horses to their harnesses, and the coaches were ready. Before she climbed in, Mistress Jane pointed to the sun. "Clarence, ain't that direction west?"

The November sun set early, and it would soon be night. I dreaded being cold and wet in the dark.

"Yes, lovely lady."

"Then why ain't we going that way to California?"

Our Honorable, stovepipe hat in hand, turned to Milo. "Clarence, couldn't we reach there faster going straight across country? Why are we heading north?"

Kentucky Bob said, "Dang fool," and climbed up on his drivers' bench. That red scar was like a thermometer.

"We follow the rivers," said Milo. "This Missouri River up to North Platte, North Platte to Sweetwater River. South Pass is the gateway through the Rockies and into Salt Lake City in Utah. From there we go into the Nevada desert, across mountains of Sierra, and into California. At least that's what they told me."

Honorable Mister Higginboom stared at Milo. "You people of labor are marvels," he said. "Here I been halfway there myself and couldn't tell you that. Of course, Zeke and the others were responsible for the trip."

"Clarence," called the mistress, "that man didn't answer my question."

Milo spoke loudly without looking at her. "We follow rivers because twelve travelers and twenty horses have to drink. And ain't nobody can carry enough water for them."

Mistress Jane slammed the door to her coach.

"Let's start rolling, men," called our master. "I feel as though we're almost there."

Milo turned and spit. His contempt echoed from each of us. After a few moments of despair I mounted Pretty Girl. Milo showed Kentucky Bob how to have his team pull the coach uphill at an angle.

"You don't want the coach to tip over," he called.

Coaches could tip over? Seth and then Caesar followed

with their teams and coaches. I asked Eliza for blankets for me and Chloe. We folded them into shawls to tie around our shoulders because the air was damp and cold. My fingertips, ears, and nose were freezing.

When the coaches were on the trail, Chloe and I rode up. When Milo waved, we cantered ahead of the first coach. Everyone was tense until Seth began singing. We stayed close enough to join in.

> "I'm on my way, and I won't turn back,
> I'm on my way, and I won't turn back,
> I'm on my way, and I won't turn back,
> I'm on my way, great God, I'm on my way.
>
> I asked my brother to come with me,
> I asked my brother to come with me,
> I asked my brother to come with me,
> I'm on my way, great God, I'm on my way.
>
> If he won't come, I'll go alone,
> If he won't come, I'll go alone,
> If he won't come, I'll go alone,
> I'm on my way, great God, I'm on my way.
>
> I asked my sister to come with me,
> I asked my sister to come with me,

I asked my sister to come with me,
I'm on my way, great God, I'm on my way.

If she won't come, I'll go alone,
If she won't come, I'll go alone,
If she won't come, I'll go alone,
I'm on my way, great God, I'm on my way.

I asked my boss to let me go,
I asked my boss to let me go,
I asked my boss to let me go,
I'm on my way, great God, I'm on my way.

If he says, 'No,' I'll go anyhow,
If he says, 'No,' I'll go anyhow,
If he says, 'No,' I'll go anyhow,
I'm on my way, great God, I'm on my way.

I'm on my way to Freedom Land,
I'm on my way to Freedom Land,
I'm on my way to Freedom Land,
I'm on my way, great God, I'm on my way."

I watched the trail and I watched the rises. Chloe saw a deep hollow, and we warned Kentucky Bob. Seth's and Caesar's coaches always followed his.

It grew dark, and Chloe and I were alone ahead of the teams. Solomon was sleeping in Caesar's coach.

"Jacob," she said.

"What?"

"There be Indians behind those trees."

10

Indians watched us day after day. Whether they were the same ones or new ones, I didn't know. As the teams pulled better we settled into dreary ten-hour days. We ate biscuits at morning, had two watering times for the horses, and then had our cooked supper. Evenings Milo and the others took the horses to graze nearby and returned them for the night to the center of the three coaches, set in a triangle.

Men and women brushed horses with currycombs; and the animals grew their thick winter coats. Milo had chosen these heavy-harness coach horses well. They were well trained, but spirited, and wore horseshoes with cleats for ice and snow.

Each night we used picks to remove stones from their feet. We picked burrs from their legs and coats and tied blankets over them. Eliza's blankets kept them warm and dry.

"Do those animals have to sleep near us?" Mistress Jane had asked the first evening. "It's like smelling a barn."

"If we want to keep Indians from stealing them, they do, lovely lady," Honorable had answered.

The mistress refused to allow Solomon near her. Hannah said, "She's afraid her baby will come to be like him." I felt angry about Solomon being kept distant, but he liked to hide under the coaches anyway.

Week by week Mistress Jane seemed less afraid of us and became a more decent person. Some days she stirred soup with Polly and brushed horses with Milo. She asked Eliza to teach her to sew a horse-blanket stitch. Honorable and the mistress grew friendly and seemed amazed at us.

One night I crouched behind their coach and over-heard them talking:

"Clarence," she said, "these slaves are regular people. Kind and patient. When I heard about slaves back in the country, I thought they were lower than us."

"Men and women of labor," he said. "Jane, you should have seen all of them. I didn't know as to how I would go about choosing from among one hundred or so Africans."

"At the slave house?"

"At an outdoor auction. These slaves were barefoot on cold, wet grass. Ten shiny faces standing still as stones in running water. Waiting. They were, well, together, you know?

"I just felt a voice calling, 'Buy them, Higgins.' After I

purchased them, I felt so proud. As a rich slave owner, I needed a noble name. I chose Higginboom because just then the clock boomed. Higginboom. Don't it sound great?"

"But, Clarence, you shouldn't have paid for the boy who's sick in the head."

"Jane," he said, "it was strange; they were gathered around him. First the women, then the other boy or girl would hold his hands, and I had a special feeling about him. He's our good-luck card."

"But, Clarence, he frightens me."

"Now, now, lovely lady Jane, don't you worry none. Our baby will be fine."

That's what I heard Honorable and the mistress say. It solved the question about his name and made me feel better about them. I felt pleased that Honorable liked Solomon.

This trip was filled with surprises. I hadn't expected sunrises and sunsets to be so glorious. It seemed the entire sky exploded into burning when the sun rose or when it said farewell before it slipped below the flatland. I'd find myself holding my breath until I felt dizzy. Just looking was a hallelujah prayer. When the sun left the sky, I'd find tears in my eyes.

It was chilly riding Pretty Girl, but I had been cold in winter all my life. Our last master kept us barefoot. He told us it was to remind us of the position in life God wanted for us. Caesar said wasn't God who wanted it, but Master.

However, I could hardly believe that now I wore thick socks and sturdy shoes. My winter underwear, woolen suit, and blanket were warm too.

And we were all busy.

On the trail Milo was everywhere. Feeding bran and oats to the horses in the dark of morning, putting salves on their leg sores in the dark of evening. He worked so hard, Kentucky Bob insisted that Milo sleep all night. Milo was the one who knew the way and handled the horses. Somedays he was so busy watching the teams that he couldn't take bets until nightfall.

Because Milo slept, the night watch was divided among Seth, Caesar, Kentucky Bob, and me. I took the first hours from supper to midnight, riding Pretty Girl, and Chloe rode Black Midnight beside me. For night watch, her horse was well named. Shortly after midnight we woke Caesar for his watch.

When it rained, we were wet and everybody smelled like old dogs. When the sun shone, everyone dried off. Soon I felt so cold and miserable, rain or shine mattered little.

Polly, in her red head wrap, was a wonderful cook. The first couple of days her food seemed poor in comparison to the hotel food. Later on I was so hungry, her food tasted like honey from heaven. One night Polly caught me and Chloe by the hands. She beckoned to Solomon and hugged him.

"Listen, you children. It do my heart good to cook for you. I had me two sons and a girl almost grown. But while I cooked for white children at the Big House, my own children went hungry. Then Master sold my children." She wiped away tears.

"But now," she said, squeezing us, "for the first time I be cooking for brown children. Praise the Lord!"

She used molasses to make the shortening bread and biscuits delicious, and she boiled salt pork with potatoes or turnips. Chloe found where they hid the dried apples, and we chewed a few slices every night. We ate from tin bowls Hannah had bought, and we even had spoons and forks.

When I was a child, sometimes they made us eat from pig troughs. They whipped us if we used our hands, so we had to put nose and mouth down. Then the white folks would laugh and say how the pickaninnies ate like animals and how we had food all over our faces. I would grin for them, but inside I would be burning angry. Now we ate like Honorable and the mistress.

We all played important roles, ten slaves with different work skills. Milo handled horses; Caesar, Seth, and Kentucky Bob drove teams; Seth, our musician, led us singing; Chloe and I were scouts; Polly was our cook;

Hannah was our healer; Eliza mended and sewed; and poor Solomon played under the coaches with stones. I decided that he should do something.

Eliza always told me, "It ain't smart to be dumb. You need all your wits about you." So I tried to teach Solomon to gather firewood so he could be of use.

When we guarded camp, Indians kept us company. In fact, I waved once, and a boy beside a brave raised his hand. Somehow I felt that they kept the outlaws away. Were they waiting for something to happen before they stole our horses?

One morning on the trail I heard a loud cracking sound behind me and Chloe. Milo shouted, and when we galloped back, we saw him holding up the second coach.

In a second Seth leaped off the driver's seat and was beside Milo. Polly and Eliza spilled out of the coach.

"What was it?" I called.

Chloe pointed. "It be a broken wheel, Jacob." The wooden wheels were built in sections between the spokes, and two sections had cracked.

As soon as I dismounted, Solomon was beside me. He bumped me with his elbow. What did he mean this time?

Milo asked, "Who can get the spare?"

Solomon bumped me again.

"I will," I said, "me and Solomon." Caesar handed me a hammer and a wrench, and we crawled in the mud.

Under the coach I understood why Solomon had bumped me. No one else knew about those boxes of gold coins.

With hammer, then wrench, I freed the spare wheel, and Solomon caught it. "You take it," I told him, and he crawled out with it.

"Stay there, Jacob," called Milo. "I be sending one back. I want to keep this wheel. Never know."

One wheel broken, two more spares. I heard Milo's betting mind figuring the odds, but he dared not speak. I saw Eliza's muddy shoe tapping the ground as a warning.

After storing the broken wheel, I crawled out and looked around. About seventeen Indians on horses were watching us from a distant ridge. As we rode on, I felt my scalp crawl.

Sometimes the Pony Express riders' path was near our wagon trail. We'd hear the drumming of the mustang's hooves and get a glimpse of a red shirt sailing by. I would lead the cheering.

I was always thrilled, but not Honorable Mister. More than once he said, "That Pony Express is New York City trying to dictate to business in California. California don't need no eastern influence. We're westerners."

And Eliza said, "It ain't natural to ride that fast. Dangerous. If the rattlesnakes don't bring that rider down, the Indians or the outlaws be digging his grave."

But Chloe and I, we smiled at each other.

After the first couple of weeks I grew tense. "Chloe," I said one morning, "if it be November, then election day must be over." That was a day to write about for my Book of Life.

"Jacob," she said, "let's say a prayer for Mr. Abraham Lincoln." I looked down and waited, but she was silent. She looked up, and all I had time for was "Amen."

"Chloe, you didn't say no words."

"For silent prayer, ain't no words needed. Jacob, that means the election results will be sent to California any day now."

"And we should see that stagecoach driver with the green scarf and the Pony Express pay soon."

"Watch out," she cried. The trail suddenly disappeared at a riverbank. We rode in circles until we found where it had curved. Luckily, we were far enough ahead to turn Kentucky Bob's team on the right path. For an hour we traveled straight, away from the water, then to my relief I spied water again.

At the sighting of water Milo called, "Seth wins Kentucky Bob's buttons."

From her coach window Eliza called, "No cutting buttons till California."

"That's ten buttons you owe me, Kentucky," Seth called. Kentucky Bob grunted. He was a sore loser even when the gambling was for fun.

Solomon ran up and climbed on Pretty Girl. He rode

well now, and I was pleased that he had chosen to ride with me.

Chloe pointed ahead. "We can't see up there," she said.

I stared. "It be either fog or snow." I pulled my cap down as if that would make me warmer.

Solomon bumped me with his elbow. He seemed to keep his fingers for playing in front of his face, and he used his elbow to point. Of course the Indians were there on a rise in the prairie. We always saw them, but I wasn't sure the others did. I had decided not to worry Eliza or the other women.

Milo whistled for the teams to stop.

"Snow on the sixteenth day from our bet," called Kentucky Bob. "Seth and Caesar owe me five buttons each."

Chloe rode back to the third coach, and I tried to follow, but Solomon kept bumping me.

"What?" I asked.

He stared away. I sat on the horse wondering what he was trying to tell me this time.

Kentucky Bob swung down. "I think I saw me a deer in that thicket," he said. "I think it got my name on it."

Solomon allowed me to water Pretty Girl, but he kept bumping me. I tied Pretty Girl's reins to our coach so that she could reach grass and turned to him. He held out an empty flour sack.

"Who's it for?" I asked.

He turned toward the hill where I last saw the Indians. "Take cornmeal to the Indians?"

He looked at the ground. I weighed the empty sack in my hands and in my mind. Polly wouldn't approve. Milo wouldn't allow it. I would have to steal some cornmeal.

As soon as the men and women were relieving themselves in the prairie, I climbed into the second coach. I dumped some cornmeal into the sack Solomon had given me, tied the top in a knot, and stuffed it inside my coat.

When I jumped out and closed the door, Solomon and I were in a world of dancing snowflakes. However, the boy who used to lose himself in a house led me toward the Indians. I thought I should go back for Pretty Girl, but then again, my horse needed to graze.

After a few minutes I was lost in the blizzard, but Solomon walked ahead, looking down. I struggled to stay beside him. We climbed uphill and surprised two Indians, a man and a boy. With snow swirling all around and darkness coming on, it had been difficult to see.

I said, "Good evening. We want to share some cornmeal."

The man stared at it with folded arms, but the boy took it. He squeezed the sack and nodded.

Solomon and I nodded in return, then bowed. I stepped backward and fell down the hill, rolling to the bottom. I felt like a fool. Solomon helped me up, and I followed him back toward our camp.

For a while I thought we were lost. I blinked my eyes to keep snowflakes out, and even Solomon stopped several times. I'd bump into him and halt too. As we grew nearer I heard Milo's voice, and finally a lantern glowed between coaches.

Milo was saying, "We'll have to sweep snow off the grass when it gets covered. I want to keep the grain feedings down to once a day."

We heard a shot and a shout. Caesar and Seth ran to help Kentucky Bob drag a young doe back to camp.

Polly tightened her red turban, tied her skirts back, and built three huge fires. Eliza lined up knives and a saw. I couldn't watch the pretty tan deer butchered, so with Chloe, I rode in circles around the coaches.

Chloe said, "This would be perfect time for the Indians to steal our horses. We can't see for the snow, and the men're all busy butchering."

I grunted and gazed from side to side.

"Maybe I should ride in the opposite direction, and we'll cross each other's paths," she said.

"No," I said, "I don't want no Indian kidnapping you."

"I would scream and you'd come." Chloe was trusting.

"We stay together." Was I worried about her, or was I afraid to be alone myself? An hour or two passed.

And then I saw eleven men in the snow. Indians were waiting for their moment. Where had our two native friends gone?

"Ride close," I said, "there's a group of Indians."

11

Were we surrounded by Indians? If I called the men, they might get their rifles and start shooting. But this was the Indians' land. They probably outnumbered us, and they could call for others to come. Our little group could be killed by braves who would gain twenty handsome horses and plentiful supplies.

What should I do?

"I see them too," said Chloe. "There be five more over to the front."

We rode on. Between the coaches I saw that the deer had been quartered and skinned. Hannah was cutting meat into strips; Seth had ribs on a tripod rack over the fire.

Meat, horses, supplies. Maybe the Indians were hungry. Of course, they had bows and arrows, maybe even rifles, but we had deer meat. Chloe saw me looking. We rode on.

"The Pony Express riders said they shared cornmeal and made friends," she said.

I grunted. She didn't know that Solomon and I had already done that. Something more was needed. I cleared my throat.

"Can you go and ask them to share a quarter of the deer meat with the Indians?" I said softly. "I'll keep riding and see how many I can find."

"Who should I tell first?"

"Caesar."

After we passed the next coach, Chloe turned to ride through the horses. Voices around the fire hushed. No more chatter. No more laughter. I heard Mistress Jane squeal like a stuck pig, but her squeal was cut off in seconds. I could imagine Honorable Mister holding his hand across her mouth.

Suppose they didn't believe Chloe? Suppose they wanted to fight the Indians?

What would Kentucky Bob say? I knew he'd go for his gun. Would he want to share a deer he had shot? I bet he was angry. I shook my head: That was betting on a sure thing.

My circles seemed to take longer and longer. From fear and cold in the blizzard I began to shiver. Why had I sent Chloe? Why didn't I go with her? I rode faster and checked the ropes on our horses. When would Chloe return with an answer?

I continued riding around the camp. It seemed the Indians were all on one side—those I could see through thick snow, anyway.

Soon I saw Chloe riding out with a torch.

"Over here," I called softly, turning to where the Indians crouched.

Behind Chloe, Seth dragged a hindquarter and Caesar carried a front leg. By the fires I saw Milo struggle to hold Kentucky Bob's arm down. That scar was red.

Solomon sat behind Chloe on her horse.

I called him, and he slid down. Handing my reins to Chloe, I slid off my horse and stood by Solomon. I waved to Seth and Caesar.

"Over here," I said. They looked blindly into the swirling snowfall.

Taking Solomon's hand, I walked up to the Indians, more than fifteen of them by then. They started to back off.

I waved. "We shot a deer. Please accept some." I didn't know if they spoke English. I felt dumb, but I was sincere.

Chloe rode behind me, and by the light of her torch everyone could see the Indians—brown men in leather clothes standing with blankets around their shoulders.

Suppose while everyone was passing the deer meat here, other Indians cut loose our horses in the back? They could steal those between the first two coaches.

Softly I called, "Milo. The far-side animals. You and Kentucky Bob."

The Indians wrapped thongs of narrow leather around the two deer legs and dragged the meat away. As I watched them leave, I wondered if we had made friends.

Would friends steal horses from us? At least we hadn't made enemies. Caesar gave such a sigh of relief, everyone tittered in quiet laughter.

"Clarence boy, that was a good thing to do."

I felt pleased that Honorable had praised me, but I also felt cocky as a crowing rooster. "Jacob," I said, tossing my head. "Honorable Mister Clarence Higginboom, my name be Jacob. Jacob Israel Christmas."

As if he didn't understand, he stood staring at me. What could he do? With a shrug, he turned and said, "Clarence, are the horses all safe?"

"Milo, Milo Wilson. And, yes, we still have all twenty."

"Jane," Honorable said, "how is the Mistress Higginboom?"

"I be Hannah, sir, Hannah Turner. And your wife be fainted in the snow." Hannah's voice came from behind us.

Honorable hurried to his wife's side. Mistress Jane lay in the snowy grass, her face white as the snowflakes covering her dress.

With one hand, Hannah, who was kneeling, fanned her. Then with the other hand, she slapped her cheeks. "You wake up now, Mistress. We ain't got no time for you to be fainting."

She touched Mistress Jane's swollen belly. "Lordy," she called, "we got to get her into the coach."

Caesar stooped and lifted the mistress like a doll. Her yellow sausage curls bobbed in the firelight. With a moan, she opened her eyes. I think she thought Caesar was an Indian, because she gave a little cry.

"Lovely Jane, I'm right here," said her husband. "Clarence is carrying you to lie down in the coach."

Big Caesar had taken two steps. He stopped. Turning slowly, he said, "My name be Caesar. Caesar Jones." His deep voice was solemn.

"Yes, yes, of course," said Honorable. "Now carry her to the coach, Clarence."

Caesar stood lit by leaping flames. Everyone was silent. I could hear the horses tramping and neighing. The fire of broken branches crackled, and good-smelling deer meat sizzled as fat dripped off the rack.

No one moved.

"Caesar," said Caesar.

I had to grin. I had started the revolt; nevertheless, I felt sorry for Honorable. He needed to be a rich man before us, and we were . . . confusing him. We sure weren't acting like weak-minded slaves, but that wasn't what he had wanted.

So much had happened that evening: riding into a blizzard; Kentucky Bob shooting a deer; preparations to butcher and cook the fresh meat; Indians—the first American natives some of us had ever seen.

Now we slaves were demanding to be called by our own names.

"Caesar," said Mistress Jane from high in the frosty air, "will you please carry me to my carriage?"

Honorable Mister Higginboom's face was so red, I thought he'd pop a blood vein. However, Big Caesar stood still as ice, holding the master's wife while snowflakes swirled around him.

To my right Kentucky Bob had his fists clenched and wore a wolfish grin. To my left the women stood silently. Gently Chloe stepped away and mounted Black Midnight to guard the camp. I climbed on Pretty Girl and followed her.

"For God's sake, Clarence," I heard our mistress say. "They're people, and they just saved our hides."

That was the most sensible thing I had heard her say, but then she was being held. I could hardly believe that was my friend Caesar. He was usually mild, in spite of his size and deep voice, but not this time.

With a groan, Honorable Mister said, "Caesar."

I bet he never forgot that name.

12

After our watch I brushed Pretty Girl and covered her for the night with Eliza's blanket. My horse and Chloe's Black Midnight were tied by the third coach on the inner fireside, where I could hear them all night. Milo said horses talked to one another when there was trouble, such as Indians stealing. He knew how to listen in his sleep. I was learning.

The women were bustling in the dark. Polly cut meat to cook and smoke; she was preparing as much as she could overnight. Hannah and Eliza kept climbing in and out of the first coach.

I heard Hannah tell Eliza, "Ain't nobody here but me what can help that poor young girl. I feel like this baby be the most important of my life."

She sighed. "Eliza, it be such a blessing to heal, but will this baby live? And the young little mother. She ain't never had a child before."

Poor Mama seemed busy, but she could sleep during travel tomorrow. I heard Chloe climb out from the third coach, where she had been alone. She stood by the door of the second coach, where the men slept. Caesar was out guarding camp. I opened the door and slid down. I didn't want to wake Milo or Kentucky Bob.

"She's having birthing pains," Chloe said in a whisper.

"Is that good?" I asked, walking away from the coach.

"No, bad. It be too soon," she said. "Baby can't live if she births tonight."

I shook my head. We huddled by the fire.

The snow had stopped, and the whole world was covered in a cape of white. Under a full moon the whiteness was as bright as daylight. A slight wind stirred the white flakes. Snow whispered like a breath of winter, the only sound besides the popping of branches in the fire and the women murmuring.

"He'll be robbing that stagecoach soon," said Chloe.

I nodded.

"How we going to stop him, Jacob?"

Her question made me feel impatient, but I wasn't out of patience with Chloe. I was angry with myself. "I been thinking day and night," I said. "I can't figure how he plans to do it. Or how we'll stop him. He ain't done nothing too smart so far."

"Killed Zeke Hill."

"Maybe, but I wonder."

We were standing ankle deep in snow away from the coach doors and shivering. I had meant to come out for

104

only a second, after all; Chloe and I would have to ride scout in the morning.

Kentucky Bob slid out of the second coach. He stretched, then reached back for a blanket for me and a blanket for Chloe. She covered her head and shoulders. Nodding thanks, I did the same.

More and more we helped one another without being asked. Just as the horses knew one another now and pulled as teams, we were a team. We noticed one another's needs.

Kentucky Bob squatted. We did too.

"Now, I'm a man of thirty-five years," he said softly. "I done seen the best of white men and the worst. I know men who killed and men who can't kill."

I wondered if he had ever murdered anyone. There had been rumors about Kentucky Bob, but since the trip I felt I knew him better. I decided that if he had killed, it was to save someone's life or to defend himself.

He cleared his throat. "Honorable Mister Clarence Higginboom be a man who ain't able to swat a fly."

"What about his partner?" Chloe asked. "Did Zeke Hill die in an accident?"

Milo's voice called softly from the coach. "I be betting one hundred to one that the master don't know for sure what happened to Zeke Hill."

"I'll raise that bet and say there was an accident," said Kentucky Bob.

"I think he murdered him but didn't mean to," said Chloe.

We squatted in silence for a while. Chloe and I were talking with the men about Honorable killing, but they didn't know about the stagecoach robbery plans.

Before I returned to the coach, I whispered to Chloe, "Maybe he can't rob no more than he can kill. Maybe we won't have a problem after all."

I fell asleep this time.

In the morning Milo shook me awake. "You scouts have a big job today."

Outside the men were sweeping snow to let their teams graze while the women were scraping knives, pans, and racks. We couldn't find water, but snow made good washing. I washed my face and hands with snow, then wished I hadn't. I began shivering.

Milo walked around the camp muttering.

"What's wrong?" I asked.

"I had me three extra feed bags," he said. "They been disappearing one by one."

"Don't the horses each have their own?"

"Good to have extra. If one drops in this snow . . . ," he said, and shook his head.

I saw Chloe. "How's the mistress?" I asked.

"They gave her some herb tea from Hannah's leaves. The pangs of birthing stopped, but she has to lie down today."

"That be good."

"She has to hold that baby," said Chloe.

I nodded. Allow me to say that I knew women's birthing affairs were above and beyond my abilities. I could hardly take care of Mama, and Solomon, and Chloe, and the Pony Express, and California, and the Union.

Nevertheless, I often thought about that little unborn baby. I knew it wouldn't be brown, but I sometimes dreamed about a brown baby strutting in a stovepipe hat.

Milo called us. He waved. "Look at our trail."

The snow had filled in every wagon-wheel rut. Every hill and low place was the same height, filled up with drifted snow.

Milo groaned. "I be so foolish. All them stars out last night. I should have set our course by them stars. If the sun don't come out and we can't find the river, we wait."

I looked all around. Usually on a cloudy morning one set of clouds was brighter than another. This day heavy clouds were all dark, and the river had disappeared under snow.

Polly called, "Find me some twigs and roots for smoking wood. We'll use the time." Her skirts were tied back out of the snow. After cooking all night, she was still ready to work. Eliza helped her.

Hannah walked the mistress out to relieve herself. "We had a false call last night," she said. "This baby be settled down now. I done told him we ain't ready for him, and he ain't ready for us."

Honorable used a bush to sweep the snow around the first coach. "Clarence," he called.

No one answered.

"Uh, Milo?"

"Yes, sir, Honorable Mister."

"See this bush?"

"Yes, sir."

"It's sage."

"We been having a lot of sage lately."

"That's wonderful. Marvelous. We get into sage country at the Platte River. Then what do we do?"

"Go west, sir, following the river," said Milo. "We must be out of Kansas and into Nebraska now. If we follow the river, we be reaching Fort Kearney soon."

"Due west, Milo."

"Yes, sir, and where is west?"

Our master looked all around. He stared at the ground, and he squinted at the sky. Backing up, he walked past each coach.

"Ain't it the first coach what stopped first?" Caesar asked. "Don't we go that way?"

"I pulled around, and then some," said Kentucky Bob.

"Milo, head in that direction," said Honorable, pointing.

"No," called Seth and Caesar.

Seth pointed. "West be that way."

"Where's the river?" Chloe asked. As they argued she and I mounted and rode back and forth.

"Can't be frozen this soon," said Caesar.

I rode in a different direction, and Pretty Girl floundered and slid downhill. "Here's the river," I called. "I be over the banks."

Pretty Girl trotted on the surface and broke through ice. "Ain't more than a foot deep, but that's good for drinking."

I glanced back. Eliza, eyes squeezed shut, had her hands folded in prayer. Within seconds, the sun burst through the clouds. After we broke camp we headed west along what Milo called the North Platte River. Honorable of course rode in the first coach. This whole trip he hadn't ridden his black horse.

"Men," Honorable called out the door, "look out for a black stagecoach with an Irish driver. Wears a bright green scarf. I have to talk to him." He shut the coach door.

Chloe and I looked at each other. So he planned to rob that coach after all.

"By the way, Milo," called Seth. "Where else have you stored bags of grain?"

"What do you mean, where else?" Milo's voice was shrill.

"We emptied the last bag of horse feed this morning."

"No grain?" Milo yelled. "Snow cover. No grazing, no grain. How can we feed the horses?"

13

As we rode that morning my heart ached for our beautiful horses. Snow-covered grazing, no grain, and cold weather. How long could they stay alive that way? Poor Pretty Girl. My mare wasn't as handsome as Chloe's Black Midnight gelding, but I liked her just the same. I leaned forward and patted her.

Chloe said, "I've heard tales of animals—people, too—starving on the way west."

I nodded. We would all be suffering soon. We had already passed bones, but I had told only Caesar about them. He had a wise head on him. He was big but never acted rough, and he taught me how to get along in life.

"Jacob," he would say, "got to build a bridge when you meet a man. And don't burn that bridge when you leave a man."

Caesar said life was a mystery none of us was supposed to understand. Although he couldn't read, he told me that the Bible said in Ecclesiastes: "You know not the work of God which he be accomplishing in the universe."

I could tell my friend Caesar about the bones, but I wouldn't tell Eliza or Chloe or Milo. Eliza would worry; Chloe would be afraid; and Milo had enough troubles. Snow cover was one.

This trip was forcing me to grow up, to make judgments.

I told Chloe, "Maybe we can brush the snow off the grass for grazing. It ain't frozen stiff yet."

We were passing Milo on the first coach.

"Go on ahead, but slowly," he said. "Your horse will sense whether you be sliding into a hole. And, yes, we'll shovel snow off the grass for grazing. We gonna stop early for it."

Soon my squinted eyes ached from gazing at white snow. Nevertheless, with Chloe riding beside me, I felt each footfall of Pretty Girl bounce in my soul. My eyes were searching the snow, but my spirit sailed on the clouds in that big sky. Two rabbits scurried by, and we saw other footprints in the snow.

"Big dogs?" asked Chloe. We were far ahead of the coaches.

"Wolves," I said.

"Shouldn't we go back and tell Milo?"

"I reckon he sees the prints too."

The snow silenced sound. The hoofbeats of our horses sounded like the animals were on tiptoe. I looked far and near. Right and left I glanced, but Chloe saw it first.

"Jacob, what be that?"

I yelled and waved. Milo called for the teams to stop.

Snow covered the animal that looked like a short horse. It stood still, head down. As we rode closer I saw its shaggy coat.

"A mule," I said.

"Out here by itself? Where be—?" She pointed. Girls must have quicker eyes. I saw only a mound of snow, but Chloe slid off her horse and ran toward it. A dog beside the snow-covered heap rose up and snarled at her.

I heard Seth running, so I rode to reach down and pull Chloe back. The gray dog shook and snowflakes flew. Seth tried to turn Chloe's head so she couldn't see.

"No," she said, pushing Seth away, "that's a man there. Maybe we can help him. Let me go, Seth."

"Chloe, this ain't nothing for a girl to look at."

"Leave her alone, Seth," I said. "She's a strong girl." But I was glad Seth was there. All the men gathered around.

Caesar pushed the crouched body, and the dog wagged its tail. When Caesar raised the snow-covered head, the man's blue-eyed face stared at us blindly. His long black mustache touched his bent knees, and he was holding a gun against his chest.

"Frozen?" I asked.

"Dead long enough to go stiff and then soft," said Caesar.

Honorable Mister Higginboom took the man's big

Smith & Wesson revolver. "Just what I needed," he said. "Leave the dog and mule."

"Sir," said Seth, "I beg to differ. A watchdog be a great protection. Like this one was keeping him safe. See the wolf prints?"

The man and the mule had been circled by prints in the snow.

"They dared not come near this lone dog. And it be my bet," said Seth, "this dog would bark if outlaws or Indians came up to us unawares."

I saw Milo smile. The bet was on.

"A dog is great," I said, and held one hand out for the bitch to sniff. I held both our reins in my other hand.

"I can't feed that mule," Milo said, turning back toward the coaches, "but that mule might feed us before long."

Did he mean that? Did Milo think we might starve?

As Seth took the mule's reins I glanced at Honorable Mister. His slaves had made the decisions and disobeyed his orders. How did he feel about it? I couldn't tell, and nobody else waited to find out. Slaves on my last plantation had been shot or sold for such disobedience, insubordination.

I felt strong, smart, capable, and I had never felt that way before.

Seth led the mule away, but Caesar and I lingered by the crumpled corpse. Caesar said, "Ground be too frozen to bury him." Solomon had already begun to gather rocks. We tried to lay stones over the body; but it wouldn't be long before wolves scratched those rocks away. We left the dead man.

As we walked away the dog stopped, whined, and looked back. When Caesar rubbed behind his ears, she licked his hand and came with us. Eliza met us with deer entrails, which the dog tore apart, making the snow bloody as she ate. Eliza offered a handful of spilled oats to the mule.

"Flat on your palm," said Milo. "And watch your fingers. This mule got him some nippy teeth." He bent to look. "Young animal," he said. "Strong, short teeth. And I reckon," he said, and looked at Honorable, "that was a road agent out to rob our coaches."

Solomon walked beside me in the snow. I saw his brief smile, and I squeezed his cold hand in mine. Honorable's gold is safe, I thought.

"One less problem we'll have," said our master. "My wife is fine now, and we're on our way. Look out for that black stagecoach. We're lucky, men."

"We'll never catch up to it," Caesar said.

"No, we'll pass it," said Honorable. "It'll be headed east." He scraped snow off his shoes, opened the door, and climbed in the coach with Mistress Jane. He still had not ridden Chloe's horse. I wondered if the master knew how to ride?

Where had they come from, Honorable and Mistress

Jane? South? North? East? West? They sure weren't familiar with slaves or horses.

"Our animals might starve, and he thinks we're lucky," said Milo. He spit in the snow. I watched snow melt around his warm saliva. Kentucky Bob, Seth, and Caesar started their teams. Chloe and I mounted.

We rode toward noon.

"Not as much snow here," Chloe said, looking around.

"Not as deep," I said, feeling more hope.

"Look!"

Ahead of us suddenly the ground was dry tan grasses and sage bushes blowing in a breeze. I glanced back. Milo had fallen asleep on the driver's seat beside Kentucky Bob. I rode back at a canter to wake him, and he called for the teams to stop for grazing.

"Hillsides all around," I said. "No wonder the grass is thick down here."

Caesar put his hand on Pretty Girl's neck. "I don't like the feel of this place. Someone should guard them hills."

Chloe and I headed out. When I glanced back, the men had allowed the horses to spread out grazing. This should be their feeding for the morning, but no one could guard that space. Indians could easily stampede the horses and chase them over a hillside. Danger traveled with us, but the sun came out.

When I looked up, I wanted to raise my arms to touch that wide sky. My heart almost leaped from my chest in delight, then I felt guilty because we weren't safe.

As we rode along the ridge Chloe said, "You know, Jacob, this be the biggest land I ever did see. That blue sky, them miles of prairie. Here, I almost feel free, you know?"

So she felt the same as me.

She sighed and asked, "What will you name the dog?"

That was something pleasant to think about. "Why don't you name her?"

"I'd name her Faithful."

At first I frowned. I would have named her Wolf. She was almost as big as a wolf, and she was as gray as Pretty Girl. But then again, she had guarded her master faithfully. Of course, Outlaw would have been a great name too.

"Faithful is good," I said. "I like Faithful."

This time I saw him first. "Chloe, look."

In the distance his red shirt was bright against tan grasses and bare brown twigs. The rider was bending back and forth, almost like a red flag waving.

We galloped downhill toward rider and horse. The brown mustang was small, short of flank between the ribs and hip and broad of withers between the shoulder blades. I hadn't paid attention to the other mustangs back in Missouri. The Pony Express boy knelt bent over in a thicket of small brush.

"What happened?" I called.

"Oh, thank God," the rider said, looking up. "You'll ride the mail for me."

I opened my mouth, but nothing came out.

"You're shot," Chloe said, sliding off her horse. "Poor man, you're bleeding."

"I rode as fast as I could," he said, "but I was fainting. I had to stop."

"You," he said, looking up to me. "This is the most important mail we'll ever carry. Take it to Long Shadow Station. Only ten miles to go."

"Maybe one of our men should ride," I said. "We have three coaches over that rise," and I pointed behind me.

"No, men are too heavy," he said. "You're small. You, Jacob, ride."

I was surprised that he knew my name. I stared at him.

"Remember talking at the Patee House?" he asked. "I'm Nick."

14

"**N**ick, you're bleeding," said Chloe

He shook his head. "They're trying to stop the mail from reaching California, but you'll make sure it gets there."

"Election news?" I said, kneeling beside Nick.

He nodded.

"Who won?"

"He's bleeding, can't you see, Jacob? Don't ask about elections." Chloe put an arm around the rider.

Nick pointed. "They said they'd scratch it under the right front mail pouch. Lift that. I suspect it will read either an 'L' for Lincoln or a 'D' for Douglas."

With trembling finger, I lifted the pouch and saw a clear letter "L." "It be an 'L.'"

"For Mr. Lincoln, then. He'll be our next president. No wonder they don't want the news to reach California."

Mr. Abraham Lincoln elected president. We might be freed! My heart almost leaped from my chest. And I might get to ride the news on its way to California. This was what Chloe and I were working for. Getting the news to the West. Pay or no pay, riders would carry this news on its way by Pony Express.

I tried to pet the brown mustang, but those ears flattened, and it bucked and kicked.

"Copper, it's all right," Nick told the horse. "Mustangs can be mean," he said, "But they know how to fly. You'll see."

"I don't know the way."

"The horse knows this part of the trail. Just lean forward and stay with him. That's all you—" He groaned and bent over. His wound seemed painful. "They shot me on purpose."

Chloe said, "What's to keep them from shooting you, Jacob Israel?"

I had to think about that. "I'll cover the mochila," I said, "and I won't be in a red shirt and blue pants." However, I wished I could wear his uniform. I took off the blue blanket I used as a warm shawl.

"Keep it on," Chloe said. "You'll be cold going fast. Take mine. I can get another."

I used her dark blue blanket to cover the mochila, and I tied the ends around the mail pouches. I wanted to ask Nick about the station, but when I mounted, the horse stood high on its back legs.

"He always rears up like that," Nick called, but I could

barely hear the last word. Copper was tearing across the earth. I bent just in time to keep my head from being cut off by a tree limb. After that I stayed low on the mustang's back and held on.

I was shivering from cold and excitement. Nick hadn't told me what to expect at the station, but I'd find out. Was I really carrying news of Mr. Abraham Lincoln's election? This was what I had dreamed of; I was saving California for the Union. What a privilege.

Copper slowed to a trot in a thicket. Tree branches scratched my clothes and tugged at my cap. With one hand, I pulled my cap snug. My head was turned, my eyes were squinted to keep twigs from blinding me. On rode that mustang, and I relaxed as we came out of the woods. But some men stood by a tree.

"Boy," they called.

I kept Copper trotting. In the dull winter light I glimpsed the metal of a gun barrel. "Sir?"

"Is that the mail? Are you a rider?"

"I be a slave from a coach," I called as I pressed Copper to race on. For a while I tensed, waiting for the bullet. I was grateful that I had covered those mail pouches.

At the rate we were galloping, I'd be at that Pony Express station in about an hour. I wondered how Chloe would get Nick back to camp. He had Pretty Girl to ride. If he could mount her. Hannah would dress that shoulder wound with her ointments and herbs. Our horses were grazing, and Milo might make camp there for the night, but how would I return?

The Pony Express route wasn't exactly the same as the wagon route. How would they know where to find me? For a moment I felt panic. No, I told myself. I was racing toward a warm station with food and a relief rider. The stationmaster would know how I could return.

He might even lend me a horse, and I could ride back right away. Only a couple of hours away from Eliza. She had never liked the Pony Express. Thought it was dangerous. If I returned soon, it would ease her heart. I hoped Nick would tell Eliza that I was safe. But he had been shot!

With a moan, I cantered into a flurry of snow. Copper slowed to a trot. After a while we rode clear. Milo was right to let them horses graze now. The sky was sagging with snow.

I was so tight, I ached. Deep breaths, I told myself. It wouldn't be far now. And Mr. Lincoln would be president. Southerners wouldn't be happy, but we slaves would be. We knew how to work, and now we'd labor for pay. Have decent lives. No more whippings or insults. Chloe must be happy. Eliza, too.

Copper trotted on, then slowed to a walk. I raised my head and glimpsed a square mound on the flat Nebraska prairie. Was this Long Shadow Station? No smoke from the chimney; that worried me, but maybe a breeze carried the smoke the other way.

I hoped to find a different rider as well as a change of horse. Horses were changed every ten or fifteen miles, but riders rode one hundred miles. I remembered the boys talking.

Wind blew grass to rattle like a nest of snakes. I shivered. "Rider here," I called as Copper stopped.

No answer. No one came out to meet me.

I slid off and took Copper to drink at a trough. At least it was filled. The wooden door to the mud-brick station house was shut. I knocked, but no one came, so I kicked with my heel. No answer, but the door creaked open.

By then I was shaking like a leaf in wind. Copper, tied by the trough, was grazing now and looking back at me.

I pushed the door. "Sir, I'm here with mail."

No one answered. Now I shook like someone with malaria.

With a deep breath, I pushed the door all the way open. No windows in the station house. The only light was from the door and a shaft of light down the chimney. No fire in the pit.

I stepped inside and almost stumbled over a leg dressed in denim pants. Because of the darkness, I didn't see his face. I listened. Leaned down. He wasn't breathing; he was dead. I ran out and slammed the door.

My heart was hammering my ribs. Leaning against the door, I took deep breaths and clutched the door-frame. Slowly I walked around the outside of this small, one-room station, with no windows and only one door. In the back I saw a corral, but the gate sung open and the horses had left. Their hoofprints had pounded a path in the snow.

Should I go back and find out how the stationmaster had died? Had he been shot? I hadn't smelled gunpowder. How long ago did he die? Was he even dead? He didn't smell, but he might be frozen. I decided: He hadn't moved, and he wasn't breathing; yes, he was dead.

Some people didn't want that election news to get to the West. Did Copper know the way from here? I tried to stroke the mustang's neck, but Copper wasn't a pet.

"Boy," I said, "you have to carry me to the next station. It be up to us." I let him graze some and rest for a few more minutes. But all the time I was looking around. Suppose the people who killed the stationmaster returned?

Jumping to avoid a kick, I tied that blanket even more securely around the mail pouches. The Pony Express riders had told us how hard it was to have to ride without relief. It must have happened often since their beginning in April, and now this would be their first winter. I mounted.

More snow began to fall as Copper galloped off.

15

The sky opened, and I was lost in snow so thick, I could hardly breathe. I rode the mustang at a trot. He seemed to have a sense of direction; several times he curved around mounds. Night crept down from the clouds and wrapped us in a cloak of snow.

I sat upright now, gazing from side to side and listening. Snow stole Copper's hoofbeats so that his steps made no noise. That was good. If more people were out to stop the mail, they couldn't see or hear us. The mustang and I were a team of two, and the horse led.

When I jerked awake, I could hardly believe that I had fallen asleep. Poor Copper, he pushed forward. That horse hadn't had water or grain for hours now. Where was the next station? Were we lost?

Soon I saw a glow of light. A man stood in snow holding a lantern. What relief. I was so happy to see him, I could have wept. I wanted to yell or blow a bugle. I wanted to call, but I decided to be dignified.

The man wore an Army uniform, and he wasn't alone.

I looked forward to leaping off Copper. Brushing snow from my shoulders and head, I rode up.

I blinked. The man beside the soldier wasn't a Pony Express rider, he was fat. And old. I felt a tingle of terror. Where was the relief rider? What was wrong?

"Boy," the heavyset man called, "have you seen the Pony Express rider?"

I wanted to announce proudly, I be the Pony Express! But something stopped me: the man's voice. Where had I heard it before?

Closing my eyes in horror, I remembered. This was the man who had talked to Honorable Mister Higginboom that night. He wanted California to secede from the Union. That meant he was out to stop the election news from reaching there.

"No, sir," I answered. He didn't know me, and that meant he wouldn't recognize my voice.

"Where're you from?" said the soldier.

"Mr. Higginboom needs grain for his horses," I said truthfully.

The solider pointed. "The fort has grain."

"So Higgins has survived this far." The man laughed, and I felt angry. He was making fun of my young master. This man was supposed to be a friend to Honorable, even though they were friends on the wrong side of my beliefs. Why didn't he think we would survive? Did he want our master to die?

On Copper trotted past them. My foot held down the blanket that covered the mail pouches on their side.

I rode toward the wooden buildings that made up the fort, but I had to wonder. Should I go there? Would people inside try to stop me? I had to decide, and fast.

Did Copper know the way to the next station? I would find out. "Let's go," I said, and I turned him from the gate. He trotted faster and faster until he broke into a gallop.

I leaned forward and tried to stay in the saddle. Again we rode in and out of snow flurries, over plains and through woody thickets. From time to time I felt myself drifting, dreaming. But I stayed in that saddle.

The cold was like knives of ice. My face felt frozen, too frozen to even yawn. My eyes welled tears and my nose was running. When I tried to wipe my face with my sleeve, my arm felt stiff.

Suppose the mail arrived but I froze? I tried moving my head and shoulders. Moving let snow fill my neck, melt, and drip down my back.

Raising my chin, I stared ahead and saw light and shadowy figures of two men. Was this someone else trying to stop the mail? The older of the two wore a wide yellow scarf but no hat. The younger one was in red shirt, blue pants. The Pony Express rider had one hand out and one hand on his mustang. Copper slowed to a walk and allowed me to slide off.

So stiff was I that I fell in the snow.

"It's Copper all right, but who's riding him? And where's the mail?" called the rider.

As the men helped me up, I pulled the blanket off the mochila.

"They shot Nick," I mumbled. My face was so stiff, I could hardly speak. "He asked me to ride."

"Is Nick dead?" the rider called.

"No," I said, "he'll be all right. He be with our coaches."

Without another word, the rider swung the mochila onto the relief mustang and galloped away. The station-master supported me.

"There now," he said, "why don't you go into the station and warm up?"

The building was one story, mud and straw brick, with two chimneys, two doors, and glass windows. Smoke rose from the chimneys, and I smelled ham.

"Please, sir," I said, "can I help with Copper? He carried me here. All this way."

We led the mustang into a barn with other horses. They seemed to whinny their greetings. As Copper ate from a feed bag I brushed him and dried him off. How pleased I felt that the horse allowed me to touch him.

Night was breaking into day in the east a few minutes later when we left the barn. That meant I had ridden through the afternoon and all night.

"Come on, boy," said the stationmaster. "You need food and rest yourself."

We walked into the warm, well-lit station house. A front room was closed to other rooms by three doors. "You're colored," he said.

"Black and a slave, sir," I said. "And I have bad news."

"Bad news? Being a slave and Nick shot is bad enough. Is there something else?" Smiling, the man patted me on the back.

"Sir," I said, "at Long Shadow Station the man was dead."

The stationmaster had been adding a split log to the fire. He turned to face me. "Tom Jones is dead?"

"Yes, sir. He was on the floor. The door was closed; there was no fire in the hearth and no horses. Someone had opened the corral."

"Tom dead. Poor Tom. I wonder what happened. You rode Copper to Fort Kearney, then." He leaned against the stones over the fireplace. "Why didn't you stop there? You could have gotten help. They have soldiers to guard their relief horses."

"Yes, sir, but I recognized a man there who wanted to stop us. He was standing with a soldier."

A wave of pride almost overcame me. In spite of enemies, and with God's help, I had delivered the mail to safety. California would get the Lincoln election news.

"The man with the soldier? I had seen him before, sir.

I know that he wants California to secede. And with that blanket covering the mochila, they couldn't tell that I be riding the mail, so Copper and I rode on."

The man stared at me; he shook his head. "You rode all night, then. Good for you. By the way, they alerted us to expect trouble. Was news of the election in the mail?"

"Yes, sir."

He took a deep breath. "I don't suppose you know who won?"

"Yes, sir," I said, "it was Lincoln. Nick said they'd scratch an 'L' or a 'D' on the leather. I read 'L' for Mr. Lincoln."

The stationmaster's smile was like a sunrise. "Good."

"Sir," I asked, "when the people in California learn that Mr. Abraham Lincoln won, what'll they do?"

"Oh, I suspect they'll be loyal to the Union. The Americans and newspaper writers always did want to remain. It's mostly the Spanish and Mexicans who want a separate state under the Confederacy.

A group called the Knights of the Golden Circle even want a separate Republic of the Pacific. But we don't have to worry now. California will pledge loyalty to the president."

And the North gets California's gold, I thought, smiling. I felt like dancing. Jacob Israel Christmas helped carry the news to save the West for the Union.

The stationmaster, Mr. Bill Smith, piled fried ham and

buttered hominy grits on my plate. By the time I finished
eating, I could hardly hold up my head.

"Undress and get under those blankets," the man said.
"I'll wash your clothes." Bunks lined the walls of the
room.

Suppose Indians set the station on fire and I be bare
body? I thought. Would I have to run out into the snow
naked? But I didn't wonder long. As I dozed off, I heard
when another Pony Express rider, headed east this time,
got his relief horse and ham sandwich from the stationmaster. After that I slept twelve hours straight.

When I woke up, the room was full of Indians.

16

As I opened my eyes I spied a tub of water by my bunk. Lines were strung across the room. Mr. Smith had washed and hung not only my underwear, but my wool suit and blanket as well.

"Everything's dry, Jacob," Mr. Smith said. "I've drawn water for you to bathe in."

The scene almost matched my imagination earlier: I had been afraid that I would be bare body before Indians, and I was. I crawled from under the blankets. As I stepped into the cold water I thought the Indians made remarks about me. Sliding down, I sat scrubbing my feet when one young Indian touched my arm.

Mr. Smith said, "He says you're not pale white, but brown, like him."

I smiled and the American native smiled. We were brothers in brown. I hadn't thought about that before.

Dried and dressed, I felt like a new person. I suspected that I smelled better, too. My wool pants, jacket, and flannel shirt had been smoothed out by hand. They were only slightly rumpled from cold-water washing.

When Mr. Smith talked to me, I noticed that a couple of the braves seemed to be listening. They understand English, I thought, and I was glad I had been polite to the Indians we had met. This sitting by a fire with Indians would be written in my Book of Life.

Mr. Smith served his friends sliced ham wrapped in pancake circles of corn bread. The eight Indians talked to him, and he answered in their language. When he saw my surprise, he touched one man.

"Jacob," he said, "I was married to this man's sister for twelve years. They're Shoshone. Without their protection, I wouldn't be alive today." He sighed. "My wife died. I lost her and our son to scarlet fever."

"Yes, sir. I be sorry, sir."

I knew I probably shouldn't but I asked, "Was it hard being married to an Indian?"

He shrugged. "At first I was busy teaching her my customs. Then I learned to listen to her ways. No, being married to her was the best thing that ever happened to me." He murmured, "Years lit by sunshine and starlight."

"What did you learn, sir?"

"They live in small bands of family size. Live on the land, under rock shelters, windbreaks. Good people. No sense of wealth, no big chiefs lording over others. All members are equal and respected. Quite a lesson I learned from them."

"Yes, sir," I said. "Indians have been watching us all the way from St. Joseph, Missouri." I wanted to tell him how Solomon and I had shared cornmeal and how we all shared that deer Kentucky Bob shot. I didn't tell him. It might have sounded like bragging.

The station was warm and pleasant, but how would I get back to Eliza and the others? I hadn't asked leave of the Honorable Mister Higginboom, so I was a runaway slave, really. I hoped Chloe and Nick had explained. I didn't want any trouble.

I washed pots and wiped the wooden table. Seeing a stick with straw tied on, I swept the station floor. Mr. Smith went out to pass food and a fresh mustang to another rider. More mail.

Two Indians dozed on bunks like mine, and the other six sat by the fire talking and laughing. They seemed so human. When we slaves had a fire, we sat by it spinning stories. I'd have to let the others know about this. Somehow I had always thought of "Indians" and "warpath" together, but they could be peaceful.

When Mr. Smith returned, I said, "Sir, how can I get back to the Honorable Mister Higginboom's coaches? They probably haven't reached here yet. Since our horses are out of grain, they have to let them graze often."

He frowned. "It's good that snow hasn't crusted over the grass yet. You're pulled by horses?"

"Yes, sir. Twenty horses in all."

"What fool would bring horses out here in cold weather? Oxen and mules can hardly survive these western winters."

"Yes, sir."

"I suppose you're in covered wagons. Ten wagons, I would guess from that many horses."

"No, sir. Three coaches pulled by six horses each."

He shook his head. "That's fine for a stagecoach in the East. They have relief drivers and fresh horses. But in the West that's crazy."

Should I tell him that Honorable wanted to travel in comfort? I decided against it. Mr. Smith left, and I had to think about returning. Could I walk? But the land was large, and I could miss the three coaches and wander forever. While I thought I kept myself busy sawing firewood.

When Mr. Smith and two Indians returned from letting the horses run in the corral, he said, "Now, about returning."

What a relief; he hadn't forgotten.

"Running Deer has agreed to take you to the wagon trail tomorrow. That'll be soon enough."

The next morning after dressing and eating, I wrapped my blanket around my shoulders and put on my cap. All eight Indians seemed ready to leave.

"By the way, you said your horses were out of grain?" said Mr. Smith.

"Yes, sir."

The Indians helped him load long sacks of feed grain across their horses.

"This should get your horses through to the Fort Laramie trading post in Wyoming," said Mr. Smith. "Your master should be able to buy grain there."

Calling thanks, I rode behind Mr. Smith's brother-in-law on a horse that was a Spanish stallion. The white horse was high and powerful. I noticed that the Indians rode on the ridges. That way we could see for miles across the snowy land.

Since I couldn't speak their language, I trusted that the stationmaster had told them where to look. Two of the Indians seemed to know English, but for some reason, I felt shy around them. I thought about Honorable and the mistress. They must have felt strange at first around us slaves.

We traveled in single file for miles.

Before I saw our group, I heard our teams shaking their harnesses. The three coaches were lined up traveling in a snowy bowl. Would the men shoot at my Indian friends? Had they seen me? Shouting, I raised my arm and waved.

17

I had to let them know that these Shoshones on horse-back were bringing me home. I shouted, "Eliza, I be here." I saw her wave from a coach window. The teams stopped. Honorable leaped from the first coach and stood staring as if he hadn't heard me.

I pointed for Running Deer to take me toward Honorable Mister, who carried that outlaw's fat revolver.

"Honorable Mister Clarence Higginboom," I called loudly and slowly. The ridge echoed my voice. "Why're you carrying that gun? These people are bringing me back."

He recognized me and smiled.

"Milo," I called, "I got us oats for the horses. My Shoshone friends be carrying it." I was proud to call their name. The small band of Indians rode slowly past Honorable and toward our coaches.

Kentucky Bob, Caesar, Seth, and Milo came to meet me and bowed to the Shoshones. I swung down when we were by Eliza, and I hugged her. "Is Nick all right?"

From a coach he called, "I see you reached Mr. Smith. Devil's Breath Station. I'm well, Jacob."

What a story I had to tell him! I could hardly wait.

I ran and took Chloe's hand. I really wanted to hug her, but that wouldn't have been proper. "Where's Solomon?" I asked.

She pointed. Solomon stood, stones in hand, staring at the white stallion. How could he find stones under all that snow? I hugged him, but he barely moved. I think he was glad to see me, but he didn't show it. He hadn't changed.

"Let's load this grain," called Milo, and the men surrounded the Indians' horses. They removed the sacks of feed to store in our coaches.

I said, "Thank you," and waved good-bye to my Indian friends. As the men carried the grain, I told Chloe and Nick a little about the mail delivery and Mr. Bill Smith's relay station. Nick was interested, but Chloe was so quiet, I decided she was jealous. Didn't she realize she was only a girl?

I had worried that Honorable would scold me for leaving without permission, but he said nothing. Even though Chloe didn't say anything, to ride scout with her again was wonderful.

The next day as we rode she talked.

"Nothing exciting's done happened for us," she said. "The second coach hit a rock and turned over. Your friend Caesar helped right it, but a wheel was broken. Solomon freed the spare wheel."

"Nothing happened? That was a lot. Two wheels broken and only one more spare," I said. As I spoke I wondered what odds Milo gave us now.

"Milo be angry that he didn't bring enough grain. Kentucky Bob be disgusted because we gave away the deer meat and furious that he rode scout by himself while Milo drove his team."

Chloe turned to me. "I wasn't going to scout with that man. Faithful dog and me curled up inside a warm coach."

I didn't blame her, so I nodded.

"Our ham, salt beef, and bacon supplies all be gone, even the deer meat. We had potatoes one night, just potatoes. And they're almost gone. Caesar tried trapping rabbits and caught two. Polly made a good-tasting stew, but it was mostly water and barley."

We were silent for a few minutes.

"Well, Mr. Abraham Lincoln as next president is good news," I said. "Did you tell them?"

"No. Are you sure they elected him, Jacob?"

"You saw the 'L' for Lincoln."

"Honorable Mister be thinking Mr. Stephen Douglas won."

"Let Honorable think whatever he needs to think." Should I tell the others the most important news in our lives? Chloe hadn't done it. Maybe I should wait?

Suddenly we heard a yell behind us from the first coach. Milo called for the coaches to stop, and our master leaped out with his Smith & Wesson. As we turned to watch he ran to each driver and said something.

"Jacob, look. Here comes a coach, a black stagecoach." I had been studying the snow-covered trail. When I looked up, I saw the coach, and my heart felt squeezed against my ribs.

Even from a distance, I spotted that bright green scarf. We cantered back. What had Honorable told the men? The news of Mr. Lincoln's election was on its way, but the Pony Express riders still needed their wages.

Chloe called, "This be the robbery. What're we going to do, Jacob Israel?" Her voice trembled.

"Maybe he won't rob them," I said. I felt so helpless.

"But he's carrying that big gun."

"Maybe he'll ask." That sounded addlebrained even to me.

"At gunpoint? That means robbing," she said.

I asked, "Don't they have someone riding shotgun?" All stagecoaches with money carried protection, I had heard.

"If they do, they'll kill our master. Then what, Jacob?"

"Are we sure?" I asked. I sounded helpless and weak because I was. I couldn't think of a thing to do.

Chloe said, "Jacob, do something!" And in her voice I heard her unspoken words: If you don't, I will.

I felt frantic and shook in my saddle. It was up to me
to stop this robbery, Chloe couldn't do it. Somehow I had
to get between our master, his gun, and this Irish stagecoach driver.

Should I wrestle Honorable for the gun? Throw a
stone at him? He trotted across the prairie toward the
stopped stagecoach. From a distance he looked like a gray
ghost in the dead grass.

My teeth began to chatter, and Chloe was looking at
me. Maybe it was all just a misunderstanding. I decided to
find out politely; after all, he was our master. And Milo
had said that he couldn't swat a fly.

"Honorable Mister Higginboom, sir," I called loudly
and slowly, "are you gonna rob that coach?"

Turning, Honorable looked at me in astonishment, and
his face reddened. Had I shamed him? Was he angry?
Chloe galloped from my side and rode toward Kentucky
Bob.

"What'd you say?" called Kentucky Bob. Chloe must
have told him that Honorable was going to rob the stagecoach. I spied her waving her arms riding to each of the
coaches, and talking. I saw Eliza look out, then duck back
inside her coach.

Caesar shouted, "I ain't backing up no stagecoach robbery." He stood and lowered his gun. "My rifle be down,"
he called.

I hadn't noticed that the men were holding their rifles.

"Mine too," called Seth. "We be honest slaves here. No need to rob nobody nowhere."

Honorable Mister Higginboom staggered and turned around, his back to the black stagecoach. His three drivers stood now with bare hands raised. Honorable circled back to stare at the man in the green scarf.

Next our master walked to a low rock between us and the black stagecoach, and he sat down in the snow. Gun dangling from his hand, he shook his head between his knees. He seemed more sad than angry. At the front there was a flurry of blue skirt coming around the first coach.

"Clarence," his wife called, "don't you do no robbing work for them thieves. Them California rascals are big liars. We living an honest life now. You come on back here."

How big she looked wobbling through the snow. She was very much in the family way.

I turned and saw that Honorable Mister had waved the black stagecoach to continue. He was trudging back toward his wife. In one hand he carried his hat, in his other the revolver. Shoulders slumped, he walked with his head bent to look at the snowy ground.

"I can't do nothing right," he began, and sobbed, wiping his eyes with the gloved back of his gun-toting hand. I jumped because he might fire that gun. "They were counting on me. I might have been the first president of the Republic of the Pacific. Now I'm a failure."

Ducking behind Caesar's coach, I hid. I hoped

Honorable would forget who had called him and stopped that robbery.

Mistress Jane met her husband. "Clarence," she said, hugging him, "you're the bravest man I ever did know." I peeked at them. Arm in arm they walked back.

Honorable and Mistress Jane climbed into their coach, and Milo beckoned to me. Kentucky Bob, Seth, and Caesar pulled my reins, and I rode Pretty Girl behind the third coach. Chloe trotted up to us on Black Midnight.

Caesar asked, "What'd you mean about robbery?"

"How'd you know?" said Kentucky Bob.

I took a deep breath. "It be back in Missouri. Solomon and I overheard some men tell Honorable to rob that stagecoach. The cash he was going to steal was for paying the Pony Express riders."

I saw Solomon, hiding behind the coach, listening to me.

"What?" said Kentucky Bob. "And he was using us to back him up?" His shoulders were hunched and his hands fisted.

"He told us to hold our rifles on our knees," Milo said.

Seth said, "He would have gotten his stovepipe head blown off his stovepipe body. Did you see the man with the rifle inside that stagecoach?" He shook his head. "Wait till I tell the women."

As they parted to drive the teams Big Caesar patted me on the back. "You saved Honorable's life and his honor. Good job, Jacob."

Our teams pulled the coaches forward, and Seth sang to soothe us. Chloe and I scouted ahead, but we sang with him. Some tense moments had passed, and I felt guilty and triumphant at the same time. We all joined in harmony on "Jacob's Ladder":

"We are climbing Jacob's ladder,
We are climbing Jacob's ladder,
We are climbing Jacob's ladder,
Children of the Lord.

Every rung goes higher, higher,
Every rung goes higher, higher,
Every rung goes higher, higher,
Children of the Lord.

We have toiled in the dark and danger,
We have toiled in the dark and danger,
We have toiled in the dark and danger,
Children of the Lord."

From then on Milo fed the horses oats both night and morning. "I don't want them horses running thin," he said. "In this snow they be needing that fattening grain."

One night we guided the horses to the river and broke ice for their drinking. Skirt held up, Mistress Jane took her evening stroll across the white ground with Hannah.

To help Polly, she stirred a pot of thin potato and barley soup that was our supper.

I heard her tell her husband, "Clarence, it's as though that Hannah takes the place of the mother I never knowed. Zeke raised me the best he could as a brother, but Polly and Hannah are as sweet as molasses."

So she had a brother named Zeke? Had he been Honorable's partner, or were there two Zekes? Was her brother dead? She liked Polly and Hannah; I wished she would like Solomon.

After eating, Milo visited the men. Last of all he came to me and Solomon. "I be betting that Higginboom baby get itself born in two days. What you bet, Jacob?"

I had noticed that Seth had shaken his head when Milo approached him earlier. He refused to bet. The loss of his wife and child made him nervous for the mistress.

"She feels better tonight," I said, glancing to where Honorable Mister and our mistress sat in the doorway of their coach.

Suddenly tiny snowflakes began to dance by moonlight. It was so gentle a moment that Milo and I looked up quietly.

The lumpy sky was rolling in clouds as gray as a dead man's face, but the snowflakes seemed to bless the earth with new hope. As the snow slid off our warm faces we were silent. I wondered what the others were thinking.

Only the leaping, crackling fire dared speak. The sage

that was burning smelled sweet and spicy. But Milo wasn't kept from betting for long. "What you bet?"

"A boy," I said.

"We don't take that bet till she be in birthing time."

"Well, anyway," I said, and I looked at Hannah. She had gone to the river and returned with extra water to boil. Honorable Mister and the others already had coffee, and the soup pot was finished. Why was Hannah boiling more water?

Mistress Jane sat rubbing her back. Her yellow curls bobbed as she talked with her husband. He sat with his curly brown hair graying in the snow, his stovepipe hat on the ground. That meant that he felt low indeed. When his spirits were high, he strutted around wearing that hat.

Rubbing her back . . . our mistress was rubbing her back.

Mama had mentioned a backache. She had told me that on the Christmas Day when I was born, she felt better than she had in weeks. She had hemmed the skirt of a ball gown for her mistress, but her back ached. It was while she was rubbing her back that she knew I was coming. And I squeezed out after only one or two birth pangs.

"Milo," I said, "I bet you your first pay when you be free that that baby boy come by morning."

"It be a true bet," he said. He frowned and looked at Mistress Jane. "First pay," he said.

The mistress trampled fresh snow walking with Honorable Mister. Next she walked with Polly, the cook, her arm around Polly. Leaning shoulder to shoulder, she then walked with Hannah. I squatted by the warm fire watching her, then I went to Chloe.

"Time to ride," I said. We took our watch until the moon was at midnight; then Caesar rode and Chloe went to bed.

Outside her coach door, I called softly. "Chloe."

"What?" said Chloe. I noticed that Polly was awake and busied herself building up the fire.

"You should come out."

"I be sleepy, Jacob."

"All right. Are there any more pieces of apple?"

She opened the door and gave me four slices of dry apple. "Them be the last ones. Good night, Jacob."

"Good night, Chloe, but don't tell me I didn't call you."

Climbing into my coach, I curled up on a bag of grain. When the quarter moon reached early morning, I heard one moan, then a baby cried. I turned over and fell asleep, wondering whether or not I had bet on a sure thing.

18

The next morning Honorable Mister asked us to gather outside. I stood by Pretty Girl with all ten of us slaves. Nick stood with us.

Of course, we all knew what Honorable wanted to say. Since Hannah, Polly, and Eliza looked happy, I knew our mistress and her baby were well. It was just a matter of whether it was a boy or a girl. Seth's eyes were red, but he was smiling. Faithful dog sat in snow at Big Caesar's feet and wagged her tail.

"Men and women of labor," Honorable said, raising a gloved hand, "I have an announcement." He wiped his eyes on a sleeve and couldn't talk no more for a while.

Now I felt choked up too. Truly this was a wonderful thing. A new life had been birthed. What could I do to honor this tender moment? I removed my cap.

To my right and my left the men removed their hats. Chloe took off her bonnet, and the women followed. Polly unwrapped her red turban, and her braids were white. I had never seen her hair before. When Honorable glanced at us, he removed his stovepipe hat and sniffled like a scared kid. He looked up.

"We have a baby boy!" he shouted suddenly.

We cheered, but he waved for quiet.

"And," he said, "we have a baby girl!" We were silent.

Snapping around, I looked at Eliza. She nodded yes. I felt dizzy. I turned to Hannah. Would two babies be all right?

Honorable Mister Higginboom turned to Hannah too. She said, "They be big enough to have a hold on life."

Right away Seth said, "In all this cold them babies need a warming stove. Polly!" he called.

"You got it," she said, turning to the cooking pans.

Hannah went on: "We got to settle somewhere for the winter, though." Milo looked pleased to hear that.

I spoke softly. "The stationmaster said we'd get to Fort Laramie in Wyoming soon. They have supplies for buying."

"There's even an inn at Fort Laramie," said Nick. "You could stay there until spring."

I could sense the relief among us.

"How far to Fort Laramie?" Honorable asked.

Nick frowned. "A few weeks, with good weather," he said. "We Pony Express boys ride south of there, so I don't know for sure." He added, "I'm all better now, so I think I'll join the Pony Express below the fort."

From her coach Mistress Jane called, "Clarence?"

"Yes, lovely mother," he said.

"Where's the Sweet Water River?"

"It's beyond Fort Laramie," said Nick.

She was silent inside the coach. I heard the babies crying, and Hannah went to stir barley water for the mistress.

"Jane," Honorable Mister said, "don't you worry your sweet little head."

Putting on hats, we all moved to our work. As I led Pretty Girl to drink, Milo said, "My first pay be yours, Jacob." He was an honest gambler.

Polly handed Seth a square biscuit pan with a slotted cover. "Take this and make yourself an oven."

While I stood wondering how a fire would burn in the deep pan, Solomon ran off and returned with rocks. Poor Solomon.

"Boy," Seth said, "don't you know rocks don't burn?"

"But they hold heat from sticks and roots that do burn," Polly said. "The boy's right."

I dug up root clumps and plant sticks. Soon they smoldered, heating the rocks on the bottom of the pan and smelling of sweet herbs. The slotted cover allowed air for the fire, and sure enough, Seth had a little oven. Hannah took it into the mistress's coach.

I looked at Solomon. "That was good," I told him. His smile glimmered, then he began to bend back and forth.

I missed being with Solomon. Ever since riding the

mail, I hadn't walked with him. Whenever I was free, he was stuffing stones in his jacket or hiding under the coaches.

Our teams rolled on.

Day after day the snow grew deeper, the horses pulled slower. Nick's word, "with good weather," tolled in my memory like church bells for a funeral. Weeks of bad weather passed. Chloe rode on the frozen river's edge, I rode on the land, and together we guided the teams. Some days snowdrifts were almost as high as Pretty Girl's belly.

One evening Eliza called me and Chloe and pushed us into the first coach. We closed the door and knelt in the warmth. Hannah and Mistress Jane each held a pink gurgling baby with arms and legs waving. They reminded me of kittens or puppies. I watched as they were washed with warm water, patted dry, dressed in gowns Mama had sewn, and wrapped for nursing.

They had dark eyes and white, wispy hair. At the sight of them my heart almost burst with tenderness.

"What be their names?" Chloe asked.

"Clarence and Jane," said the mistress. No surprises there.

Throughout these weeks of our journey the babies were warm and growing, the wheels all held, and the horses had grain. However, we travelers were always hungry. One night the soup was thick.

"What be in it?" I asked Polly.

Nick laughed. "We call it wolf mutton," he said. "Boiled horse feed. I've eaten it before."

Milo grumbled, but we all had full stomachs that night. And while the snow was deep, we could still break ice out on the river. What would happen when the water froze solid?

Soon the land seemed to change. Big rocks blown bare of snow were on either side of the path. I stared at overhangs, looking for Indians. Were they starving too?

Kentucky Bob and Caesar went hunting every night, but the deer escaped them. Seth and Caesar set traps at dusk and took them up empty at dawn.

"Them rabbits got tunnels in the snow," Caesar said. "We ain't got nothing to offer them better than the grass and berries they hid."

My fingers and hands were cracked and bleeding. How I wished for Honorable's gloves. Chloe's lips were chapped and bloody. Eliza warned her to stop licking them, and Hannah gave her ointments. It was so cold, our dog Faithful rode in a coach.

In all of this, one thing was pleasant: Seth sang in his sweet tenor voice. We all joined in. His wife's name had been Mary, and this was his favorite song:

"Oh, Mary, don't you weep, don't you mourn,
Oh, Mary, don't you weep, don't you mourn.

152

Pharaoh's army got drownded, Oh, Mary, don't you weep.
If I could I surely would
Stand on the rock where Moses stood.
Pharaoh's army got drownded, Oh, Mary—
Moses stood on the Red Sea shore,
Smitin' that water with a two-by-four.
Pharaoh's army got drownded, Oh, Mary,—
God gave Noah the rainbow sign,
'No more water, but fire next time!'
Pharoah's army got drownded, Oh, Mary,—
One of these nights, about twelve o'clock,
This old world's gonna reel and rock,
Pharoah's army got drownded, Oh, Mary,—
I may be right and I may be wrong,
I know you're gonna miss me when I'm gone.
Pharoah's army got drownded, Oh, Mary,—"

One morning the snow was so deep, the coach bottoms shoveled it up, and the horses could hardly pull. Up to his armpits in snow, Milo waded beside the teams, talking to the horses. A frog could hop faster than they were pulling.

I rode Pretty Girl to the second coach. "Mama," I whispered, "pray for a break in the weather." I was ready to ride scout ahead of the teams.

She shook her head out the window. "Don't you think I been praying?"

We had ridden about four hours when I heard a yelping scream. I snapped around. Who had yelled like that?

"Higgins, Higgins, is that you? Three brown coaches, tell me it's you!"

I gazed up a hillside.

The door to the first coach swung open. "Zeke, you old scoundrel, where you been?" Honorable leaped out into an ocean of snow.

This man Zeke almost flew downhill from an overhanging cave. He was kicking up snow on either side. Twice he fell and rose out of the whiteness. Hatless, he was red of face.

I heard Mistress Jane scream, "Zeke Hill, you found us!"

Milo began counting up the bets, but I didn't even remember how I had bet. I began laughing in relief. Zeke Hill was alive! Honorable wasn't a murderer; he hadn't killed after all!

"Baby Jane Hill," Zeke called as he plowed nearer in snow.

She appeared in the coach doorway. Hands on her hips, Mistress Jane said, "Jane Higginboom, Zeke. I'm a proper wife and mother. Come see your niece and nephew."

"Babies?" cried Zeke, standing still with arms outstretched. His mouth hung open. "Sweet Mother of God, you ain't nothing but a baby yourself. My sister, Baby Jane!"

"Mother of twins, a son and a daughter," Honorable said, still plowing through snow to hug Zeke. Mr. Hill seemed at least ten years older than Honorable and the mistress were.

"I thought you'd meet us at Sweet Water River," Mistress called. "I was afraid we'd miss you, Zeke."

Hannah held her hand across the door. I knew she didn't want Mistress to step out in the snow without her shawl.

"I came back to meet Clarence. Thought you might not make it that far. This snow is bad," said Zeke. "But I'm here, I found you young rascals, and this calls for a celebration."

Milo frowned.

"I have buffalo meat, bread flour, and grazing land."

Milo smiled.

As we scrambled over a hill that was almost too steep for the horses, we saw brown grass sticking through snow only inches deep. As they drove down, the drivers had to use brakes to keep the coaches from riding over the horses. After the third coach topped the rise and rolled down with wheels squeaking, the horses were set to graze with their blankets on. Mr. Hill ordered us to gather brown lumps.

"It's buffalo dung," said Mr. Zeke Hill. He and Honorable sat on a big rock talking and watching us work. "Smells awful but burns good. You came, Clarence, in three brown coaches, like you said you would. Damn fool way to travel." He leaned back laughing. "No more oxen for us. We got away clean. Traded the gold nuggets for coins, did you?"

Honorable nodded.

Mr. Hill slapped his knee. "I told the men at Wounded Bear Bar how you would hide our gold in boxes under the coaches." He laughed. "Higgins, you did it."

So Mr. Hill knew about the gold.

Blue-eyed Mr. Zeke Hill had long yellow hair like our mistress, but his curls were tangled and matted. He sat trim and short on the rock.

Honorable smiled weakly. "You talk too much when you drink, Zeke. I had to tell folks you were dead to cover your dealings." He shook his head. "How far to this Fort Laramie? We missed Fort Kearney somehow." He adjusted his stovepipe hat.

Zeke pointed. "You're practically there, you traveling humbug. I'll slip in with you. We'll settle there until April. Who won the election, do you know?" He rested his hands on both knees.

"I'm sure it's Mr. Stephen Douglas."

"Good," said Zeke. "We'll tell them in Fort Laramie." He pointed to us. "How's it feel to own slaves, Higgins?"

Honorable turned his head. When I stared at him, he looked embarrassed. He brushed snow off his pants.

"Where's your whip to make them work faster? The

blacks are zipping right along. Seems like they obey your commands, all right." Zeke chuckled and slapped his knee. "Do you make them dance for your jollies? Christ, Higgins, we'll have us a fancy old slave plantation in California."

We all slowed down. I could sense Kentucky Bob's despair. Who could survive if we ran away now? We were helpless. In a second everything had reversed. I glanced at Chloe, she looked at me. It seemed even the horses we were bringing into the circle slowed down.

Mr. Zeke Hill slapped Honorable on the back. "I need your whip, Higgins. I want to try it on that big black one."

He pointed to Caesar, my Caesar. I felt hair rise on my neck.

"These are men and women of labor," Honorable said slowly. "They're smart, strong workers. And they've kept us alive and well."

"Good, good," Zeke said. "Do you chain them at night?"

Chains? I remembered walking in clanking chains on the road, sleeping in noisy chains in the auction house. Chains on my wrists, chains on my feet, chains across my naked chest. Anger rose in me stronger than I knew possible.

"Chains?" I yelled, "chains?" Leaping off my horse, I ran toward that Mr. Hill, but strong arms caught me.

Kentucky Bob covered my mouth, Caesar lifted me off the ground. My hands were fisted, and I was crying in their arms.

"No," said Big Caesar behind the coach, where they took me.

"Jacob," Kentucky Bob whispered, "he ain't worth the salt in the shot it'd take to shoot him."

Caesar said, "Remember the hope. When you can't rise on hope, lean into trust. The good Lord knows."

Eliza reached us running. She hugged me, and our tears mingled. Mr. Hill and Honorable were still talking. I didn't think they'd even heard me.

Our master hadn't murdered Zeke Hill, but at that moment I could have killed him. When the anger passed, I was shocked at myself. However, I wasn't the only one disturbed by Mr. Hill.

The door to first coach flew open. "Clarence!"

"Yes, lovely lady."

"Now is the time for what we agreed on." She stood in the doorway with one hand on her hip and papers in the other hand.

Honorable stood and trudged over to take them. "Zeke," he called over his shoulder, "I know you're older, but there's things I reckon you don't understand." He pointed to us. "We were helpless without them. These people are our friends now."

He called to us: "Men and women of—No," he said.

"Caesar, Kentucky Bob, Seth, Milo, Solomon, Jacob." He turned to the women: "Polly, Hannah, Chloe, Eliza."

He cleared his throat dramatically. "These are your contracts of sale. The Mistress Higginboom and me, we've written 'freed' on each and every one of them." He held them up, and I saw FREED written on the top paper.

Mr. Zeke Hill's mouth dropped open. He stared at Honorable.

Chloe held out her hands. Honorable gave the contracts to her, and she began passing them out. "Keep your freedom papers in your pockets," Honorable Mister told us, smiling.

"Fool, rascal, scoundrel, humbug dupe!" shouted Zeke, jumping up. "What do you figure you're doing, Higgins? These are my slaves too." He argued with arms waving.

Chloe hurried to hand the papers with our names on them to us. A few moments before I had despaired, and now we were free.

Free!

19

Mr. Zeke Hill stamped away in anger. When he returned with a brown leather bag of belongings, he shouted, "That's the last time you'll cheat me, Higgins."

He pointed to Solomon, who stood by the fire staring at his finger dance. "And get rid of that one. I'll shoot him for you. He's useless, you hear?"

Honorable looked away. I was glad he liked Solomon. Would he let anything happen with him? My heart ached. Didn't Solomon have a right to be who he was? How could I keep my temper around Mr. Hill? Poor Solomon.

Honorable watched as Polly fanned the fire and Kentucky Bob set up a rack over a tripod. Caesar and Seth sawed slabs of frozen buffalo meat. Mr. Hill had already skinned it and scraped out its entrails.

We were set for a feast. I saw Milo looking up at the surrounding ridges. Please don't ask us to guard, I thought. This Mr. Hill knew the land, and he wasn't worried.

We spent three days on the low-snow side of the hill. Three times a day Polly fed us buffalo with gravy and biscuits. Faithful loved the meat, and Hannah was delighted for Mistress Jane.

"Her milk be yellow as butterfat," she said. "Them babies holding on to the Lord's life now."

Night and day I slept. Milo asked us to guard the ridge once or twice, but when me and Chloe reported that there wasn't nothing moving but foxes and rabbits, he stopped asking. He slept too.

The exhausted horses and mule grazed and rested. We were letting them wander farther and farther, but there was nobody around. From morning to night Mr. Zeke Hill and Honorable fussed, but we free people could hardly believe our blessings.

"That be one thing I never bet on," Milo said one night, crouching by the fire. "To think that I be a free man." Tears brimmed his eyes as he rubbed behind Faithful's ears.

Chloe fairly danced whenever she moved. She couldn't stop smiling. "Free," she'd whisper every time she passed me.

For me and Eliza, it wasn't the same.

It was different for us because Eliza and me had been free before. We had had papers then, too. The Quakers had given the freedom papers to us. That night the bounty hunters came, Eliza handed the papers to the men. One man seemed respectful of them, but the other man took our papers. Before our eyes he tore them into little bits. "Now where's your freedom papers, Auntie?" he had said.

My hand shook whenever I remembered that night. I knew Mama was thinking about it too. But surely California would be different? And Mr. Abraham Lincoln might free everybody soon.

Our supper of buffalo meat was early the third night. As he stood by the fire our truly Honorable boss, not master, seemed pleased with himself and with his babies. "I'm the father of a son and daughter," he told his brother-in-law.

The Higginboom babies were growing. Their arms and legs were plump and their faces round. Baby Clarence had started to smile at me, but his sister still only stared with her big gray-brown eyes. My heart melted like butter at the sight of those babies.

"Higgins," Mr. Zeke Hill said, sitting on a rock by the coaches, "whatever happened to them hand sores?"

"I figured out that something in the air did it," said Honorable. He pulled off his black leather gloves, and we all stared. "See, Zeke? No sores if I keep my hands covered."

We began counting who owed who what for the bets with Milo. I grinned. Never would I have thought about Honorable having sore hands. As we whispered about it we washed the pots and bowls from supper. For the third night buffalo meat had been tender and filling. All of us workers were relaxed, but Faithful began to whine.

Seth had said that the dog would warn us if we were ever in danger. I gazed around but couldn't find anything happening. Faithful stood looking at the hills. "Good girl," I told the dog, patting her. Hair rose in a ridge from her neck to her tail, and she sat growling.

Then we heard gunshots from the ridges. Milo leaped from his coach and ran for the horses. Each man ran for his team, and Chloe and I mounted our horses and galloped around them, helping lead the horses into the center.

Six white men slowly rode toward us from six different directions. "Hands up, ladies and gentlemen," one man called, his voice echoing from the hills.

As he raised his arms Kentucky Bob swore. "Them rifles be in the coaches," he said with a groan. "None of us got a gun."

"Who they be?" Caesar asked softly.

A shot kicked up dirt at Milo's feet. He hadn't raised his hands yet because he was gathering horses. Mine were up high as I sat on Pretty Girl, and so were Chloe's. I wished she wasn't in full view on Black Midnight. I rode slowly to Solomon, pulled him up behind me, and raised my hands again. I didn't want him to get hurt.

Hannah had pushed Mistress Jane into the coach where her babies stayed warm. Both Hannah and Polly had disappeared. Could they find the rifle in their coach?

But with six men, what good would shooting do?

Eliza stood in the center by the fires with her hands high. I wished I could cover her, but Chloe and I were in the outer circle by the horses.

Four men stayed on the ridges, rifles held across their horses. Two men rode in toward the fires.

From Pretty Girl's back I saw Mr. Zeke Hill shake his head. He told Honorable, "It's Ugly Face Lane and Straight Shot Brown. You don't know them. Dead Eye Jones from Wounded Bear must have told them something."

Honorable's gloved hands trembled in the air. He kept glancing at the first coach, where his wife and babies were.

I looked there too. Would the men harm women and children? I hoped the little ones wouldn't cry. I supposed these were the "road agents" the Pony Express boys had talked about. Where was Nick? Since I couldn't find him, I supposed he was in the third coach. He knew how to shoot. But six of them?

I heard Faithful growl; she had warned us, but we hadn't paid any attention.

"Well, if it ain't the double-crossing liar Zeke Hill," one outlaw said. "You owe me, Zeke." The man was tall but thin, with a crooked nose and scars on his face.

Both outlaws laughed. "Zeke Hill, the rich man," said the second outlaw, who wore an eye patch. "Let's see if he was lying about that." The man's other eye was bloodshot brown, and his long hair was brown too.

The first outlaw swung down by the coach where the babies were. I held my breath. Chloe blinked at me. I turned slowly and saw a rifle pointing out of our third coach. Must have been Nick. But if either of these men were shot, the four outlaws on the ridges surrounding us would shoot us like ducks in a pond. Sitting high on horses, Chloe and I were in clear view.

The road agent crawled under the first coach and slid out dragging a heavy bag.

I had forgotten about the gold.

He held it up. "Gold," he yelled, and the word echoed from the snow-covered ridges.

Setting the heavy burlap bag down, he crawled under the second and third coaches. Those bags were so heavy, he couldn't carry them by the drawstrings.

From the ridge an outlaw yelled, "Let's go. Don't stay for the celebration, boys." They all roared with laughter.

The scar-faced man wobbled to his friend. "You carry two bags."

Eye Patch smiled. "Much obliged."

Carrying the third bag, Scar Face mounted his horse and rode past me through our horses and up the hill. I heard him say, "We can come back and stampede these horses. We can trade them."

I saw Milo stiffen. We were all silent as they rode off

chuckling. I listened as the hoofbeats grew distant.

"My gold, my gold," said Honorable with a moan. "Jane and the babies are safe, but my gold is gone!"

"Don't worry, Higgins," Zeke said, lowering his hands. "We can sell the slaves and horses in Laramie. We'll make it to California."

Sell slaves? But we were free! We all looked at one another. Kentucky Bob swore, but Milo called, "They're coming back for the horses. Hitch up the teams. We have to ride."

"Yes," Honorable said, "let's get to Fort Laramie, where we'll be safe."

As we took blankets off the horses and hitched them, all I could think of was being sold again. That would be my fourth sale. Eliza and me looked at each other. I knew what she was thinking: We had been through this before, gaining and losing our freedom. I knew Honorable wouldn't want to sell us, but he had lost his gold.

As I was thinking that, while everyone was scrambling to break camp, Honorable called out: "Men and women of labor, I am no longer a rich man."

From the coach the Mistress Jane called, "Clarence!"

"Shut up, Baby Jane Hill," Zeke said. "You ain't nothing but a girl. Higgins knows what he has to do."

"Zeke Hill," yelled our boss, turning on him. "You shut up. Your big drunken mouth got us robbed to begin with.

Bragging about where our gold was hidden. I have a mind to shoot you."

Kentucky Bob moved his coach forward in line. Seth and Caesar shook their heads. What could they do? Over the ridges the snow was deep and outlaws lived here. There was nowhere to run.

"My gold, my gold," said Honorable with a sob.

Solomon stared at me. Very seldom did Solomon look at me.

He grunted. Well, go, I thought. I don't have to go with you. Looking at the ground, he bumped me with his elbow.

"All right," I whispered, "I'll go with you." Maybe he was afraid to relieve himself because of those outlaws robbing Honorable. I walked away. Milo and Caesar were rapidly putting horses in harness. Good, I thought. Even if the outlaws returned, they couldn't stampede them.

Solomon stayed by the fire. I walked back to him. He turned and bumped me again with his elbow. Chloe rode over.

"Jacob Israel," she said, "he's trying to tell you something."

20

The three coaches were lined up to cross over the ridges. As I tied the mule behind the third coach, I heard the babies begin to cry. Their voices were strong now. Eliza and me tossed the hot tripod and cooking rack into a coach.

"Save that buffalo soup," called Polly. We dumped some of the soup on the ground and swung the half-full pot into the same coach.

Solomon turned around and around watching everyone. He never did that before. Usually I had to find him hiding under a coach. Standing in the open was new.

Zeke said, "That idiot boy should be shot in the head now. He don't do no work, but he's taking food from our bellies."

It was dark now and fires lit our work. Thin flakes of snow began to fall. No time to look up, everyone was busy.

First I tried to pull Solomon up behind me on Pretty Girl. He wouldn't come. He stared at me. Jumping down,

I looked all around. Cap. Coat. Had he lost something?

He bumped me with his elbow.

"What does the boy mean when he does that, Jacob?" asked Honorable. He stood, hand on the coach door, looking at us. Hannah had been right. Honorable Mister was a kind young person, not like his older partner, Zeke Hill, at all.

But I felt terrible. Solomon was making trouble, and the teams were ready to leave.

"He wants to tell me something, sir."

We had forgotten the fires, so Kentucky Bob swung down from his driver's bench and began shoveling dirt on them. One fire blinked out. I pulled Solomon again.

He yelled. Doors cracked and windows opened. Everyone in the coaches looked at us.

"What be it?" I said. "What's the matter?"

"He should be shot now," called Zeke from the first coach. "Higgins, he's holding up the teams. We got to ride."

Solomon pushed me toward the second coach. I felt embarrassed. I was so ashamed of Solomon, I wanted to hit him or shake him. And this Zeke Hill was calling for shooting him. I closed my eyes and gritted my teeth.

Taking my hand, Solomon pushed me to touch the floor of the second coach. It gave a little; the boards were loose.

Suddenly I had an image in my mind. Everyone was

out of the coaches, staring at us. Hands on hips, Eliza walked toward me. I knew what she would say.

Carefully I lifted the mat and reached in the space between the floorboards and the coach base. My fingers curled around something rough, like a feed sack. I pulled. It was heavy.

With a jerk, I held it high.

"Solomon," I screamed, "you saved us!"

Tearing open the horse feed bag, I spilled some gold coins on the trampled snow. How they glittered by the firelight!

Mr. Zeke Hill leaped out of his coach, raced up to me, and dived for the ground. "He stole my gold," he yelled. "That idiot boy stole my gold." He knelt stuffing the coins in his pockets, but I jerked the bag aside.

"The gold, the gold, I have the gold," Honorable cried. "I knew he'd bring good luck."

Mistress Jane stood in her coach doorway smiling, her curls bobbing golden by firelight. "He saved our gold," she called. She held a baby in each arm.

I cried in relief and hugged Solomon. Stuffing my hand inside the space, I felt two more feed bags. I opened them. They were filled with gold coins too.

"Three bags," I called. "Solomon saved all the gold." I pushed the feed sacks of gold safely away.

Milo smiled. "I knew I had three extra feed bags. So that's where they went."

In a small voice Eliza said, "Now maybe we be free for true." I hugged her with one arm and Solomon with the other.

"Give me that gold," Mr. Zeke Hill called, grabbing at me. He had finished picking up the spilled coins.

Mr. Hill had wanted to sell us. This gold was our fresh air of freedom, and I wasn't letting him have it.

Stepping in front of the coach door, I raised my fists and shuffled my feet. I was ready to fight that man. He wasn't getting any more gold.

Mr. Hill stepped back and turned to Honorable. He pointed to me. "The boy, the boy, whip him, Higgins!"

Honorable caught Mr. Hill by the collar. "Get in the front coach, Zeke, before I do something to you."

I turned and covered the space under the floorboards. By the light of the last fire pit, Honorable watched me, but he was frowning. Was he angry with me? I felt worried.

He said, "Jacob, if these bags have my gold in them, what did the bags they stole have in them?"

With a sigh of relief, I said, "I bet Solomon used rocks. He's been picking up stones all the way here."

Kentucky Bob said slowly, "When them men open them bags and don't find no gold, gonna be some angry sons."

"Fly, fly," cried Zeke. "Dead Eye will come after me." He ran, leaped into the first coach, and slammed the door.

"Head out," called Milo. "Watch the coaches don't be

tilting too far. We ain't got no time for an overturned coach."

When the first coach crossed the ridge, I saw that the snow was still deep on the other side. The horses in the first team struggled for footing, pulling furiously but floundering. Over three days the surface had glazed into a crust. Riding beside the first coach, I heard the snow crunching against the broad chests of the horses. Milo shared the driver's bench at Kentucky Bob's side, calling softly to the lead horses.

"Can they make it?" I asked, riding up on Pretty Girl.

"They've had three days of feed and rest," he said. "If it ain't too far, they can make it."

The lead coach broke snow for the other two coaches. Chloe and I rode beside the second coach. Eliza called, "Jacob Israel?"

"Yes, Eliza," I said. I could hardly see her for the falling snow.

"I be proud of how you care for that child Solomon."

"Thank you, Eliza. He be smart in different ways." Now Mama appreciated Solomon too.

Polly and Hannah opened the third coach window. "Solomon be our hero," said Polly, waving away the falling snow.

"He saved his neck and ours," Hannah said.

"Sure did," said Caesar, their driver.

The first team began to move faster. The horses were

pulling for all they were worth. I rode forward.

"Mr. Hill said it ain't but about five miles to the fort," Milo told me.

Chloe said, "Listen." She rode on the other side of the coaches. Now I heard calls. Sounds dimly echoing off snowflakes.

"Milo," I said, "the men are calling. They're after us."

"Tell everyone to hush," he said. "They'll look for us in the bowl first. That'll take time. Snowfall will make it hard to see. Only five miles."

Chloe broke snow to tell the second coach in whispers. I told the third coach as they passed. Somehow I wanted to sing for comfort, but I kept silent.

Snow crunching against horses produced muffled sounds. No clip-clop of hooves, no squeaking of coach wheels. Chloe raised her arm.

Yes, I heard shouts, but they were a couple of miles behind us. Of course, their horses weren't pulling heavy coaches, and we had broken snow for them. On horseback they could easily catch up with us. What would they do to us?

I waved to Milo. He stood peeking around the first coach. "Jacob," he whispered, "tell Nick to aim his rifle but not to shoot until I tell him so."

I rode to the third coach and tapped on the window. "The rifle," I told Nick.

"Are they coming?" he asked.

I nodded. How could we aim a rifle through all this snow? Milo jumped off the driver's bench and swam through snow to get his gun from the second coach. With his rifle, he crawled onto the second-coach bench and leaned out. "Can you shoot, Jacob?"

Squirrels, I thought. But to save our lives? "Yes, sir." Snowflakes were in my eyes, and I shivered.

"Climb in. Get the other side. I'll be on the roof."

As I tied Pretty Girl he climbed up and lay flat. We had four guns, and there were six outlaws. I waved for Chloe to climb into a coach too. She could tie Black Midnight's reins to the coach. But when I looked, instead of going for safety, she had ridden far ahead.

What was wrong with that girl? Was she trying to make me look bad? That wasn't being brave, that was foolish. Anyone shooting at us could pick her off easily.

I heard a whip flicking. Milo didn't believe in whipping horses, but Kentucky Bob had them galloping through snow. If only the coach didn't turn over. If only the plains were clear under that snow cover. One horse with a broken leg or one broken wheel could be our end. I knew Mama was praying, but I added my prayers too.

From the roof Milo whispered, "I can see them."

Chloe looked back, and I waved out the window toward the rear. How could I warn her? Pretty Girl trotted beside Caesar, who was driving the third coach. The outlaws heard or saw us. They began screaming and yipping.

21

"They sound like Indians," Nick said in a whisper. "Don't shoot until you can be sure to hit one."

I raised my eyebrows. Outlaws were people. Could I shoot a person?

They galloped closer and closer. Every time I looked out the coach window, they were nearer. I felt helpless inside the coach. Against Milo's orders, I opened the door and reached for Pretty Girl. After all, Chloe was still riding Black Midnight.

The snow was so thick, I could hardly see to untie the gray horse, but afterward I felt better riding. I handed my rifle to Eliza. She was a good shot. I remembered quail meals in Boston.

I dropped back to the third coach when Milo whistled. "Jacob," he said, "ride up to the front and tell Kentucky Bob to slow down. We ain't killing no horses."

I rode to the front. Ahead of me, Chloe began waving her arms. Kentucky Bob followed her path around a curve between humps of snow. Pretty Girl struggled through snow to catch up.

The first shot rang out. The outlaws had shot at us. None of us returned fire.

"Milo says to slow down," I told Kentucky Bob.

He cussed. "And let them outlaws get us?"

"He says you'll kill the horses."

He put down the whip and tied the reins to a seat post. "Get me a rifle," he said.

Honorable, who must have been listening, passed one from the coach window. Our young boss looked scared as a trapped rabbit, and that Zeke was talking fast. I took the rifle to Kentucky Bob.

The second and third shots rang out. I glanced back, but no one seemed to be hurt. The outlaws began yipping and yelling again. Kentucky Bob stood looking over the coach roof.

"Don't shoot Milo," I told him. "He's on the roof."

Chloe called and pointed.

The outlaws sounded louder and louder. They were shouting insults and cuss words, but all I could hear was snow crunching and my heart beating. None of us had returned fire.

Kentucky Bob sat down at the reins and said, "At this rate they'll be running out of ammunition before we begin shooting. Dang fools." His horses had slowed down, and Seth's horses were catching up to the first coach.

Chloe began waving her arms like a windmill. I rode ahead toward her, Pretty Girl's chest crunching through snow. Now in the whirl of blackness with snowflake whiteness, I saw a lantern. Men were opening wooden gates. A second lantern glowed inside. I saw a lookout tower and palings of wooden walls. The fort!

I turned Pretty Girl and rode back.

"The fort," I told Kentucky Bob. He drove past me.

"We made it," I said as Seth's team passed.

"We're there," I told Caesar.

Milo slid off the coach roof. "Easy on those horses," he said. "They should slow down."

I rode behind the third coach. Our mule was stumbling. Over my shoulders I was watching the six outlaws. They were still yipping.

Nick looked out the coach window. "Soldiers will ride after them. They'll think they're Indians."

After the third coach passed through the gate, the soldiers pushed the palings from each side to close it. "Were they Paiutes?" a lieutenant asked me.

"No, sir. Outlaws. Dead Eye and Ugly Face somebody."

"Dismissed," the lieutenant called to six soldiers on horseback. "It's white men."

My horse trotted behind the coaches along a snowy lane. The fort was like a walled-in town. The street was dark, but a glow from firelight shone out windows.

Soldiers knocked on the door to a large two-story

building, and when the inn door opened, cheerful, wood-burning flames lit the lane. Candles flickered in wall sconces, and fire leaped in a huge corner fireplace that opened to the inn's parlor, kitchen, and dining hall at a glance.

Our Mistress Jane and her babies were soon settled beside the fire with Faithful at her feet. Gray-brown eyes wide open, the babies stared and waved their arms at the dancing flames. We hauled clothes and supplies inside, and Eliza joined Polly and Hannah in the parlor.

Chloe and me circled back to a huge barn that welcomed our teams of horses and the mule.

"Chloe," I said as we entered the barn, "it took courage to ride ahead to the fort." Admitting it eased my jealousy somewhat.

"I had to," she said. "You be so brave riding that Pony Express. What was a girl like me to do?"

Chloe appreciated me. I smiled and put a star beside her name in my Book of Life.

For about an hour we helped the men wipe down the horses, then feed and water them for the night.

Carrying a lantern, Honorable Mister Higginboom swung open one of the creaking doors to the barn. A soldier with a gun walked beside him.

"Men," said Honorable, "I need a horse for Zeke. They, uh"—he took a deep breath—"they won't let him stay at the fort."

I grinned. That man made me lose all control. I was glad he was going.

"I want a horse and my gold," said Mr. Hill from the doorway. Another soldier pushed him in. Mr. Hill's hands were bound behind his back.

"We don't bed down with outlaws and rascals like Zeke Hill," a corporal said. "He knew better than to try to sneak in with decent people."

"Can't have none of my horses," Milo said. "The teams pull perfectly now. I'll be filing the horses's hooves and repairing them broken coach wheels while we wait for spring."

Eyebrows high, I was shocked. Whose horses were they? That was another revolt, so I joined.

"Not Pretty Girl," I said. "She be a great scouting horse."

"Not Black Midnight," said Chloe. Since Honorable had never ridden him, she thought the horse belonged to her.

"Never mind," the corporal said, "we have an old swayback mare we'll send him out on. Get moving, Zeke."

"I want my gold," said Mr. Hill with a whimper.

"You have gold, sir," I said. "Six coins, I counted them."

"See you at Sweet Water River in April, Zeke," said Honorable. When Mr. Hill was shoved from the barn, Honorable came over to me, Jacob Israel Christmas.

"Jacob," he said, "I'm going to depend on you and Solomon to hide my gold. In the spring we'll be bound for California."

He took a deep breath and looked at Milo, Kentucky Bob, Seth, and Caesar. "Thank you, men. I just heard the election news. Mr. Abraham Lincoln will be our next president. There'll be a war, no doubt. And slavery won't be extended west." He shook his head sadly.

I didn't know whether he felt sad about war coming or about slavery ending.

"But for now," he said, "you'll each have a military cot of your own to sleep on and good food. Until April."

I needn't have, maybe shouldn't have, but I felt bold. I said: "Honorable Mister Higginboom, now that we be free, shouldn't we get paid?"

He looked surprised, almost as shocked as he had been when we had wanted him to use our proper names.

We former slaves had changed during this trip. With his help, we had taken on responsibilities and thrown off shackles of mind and body. As we had sung with Seth we had been on our way to Freedom Land. Before our master gave us our liberty papers, we had broken the chains ourselves. All of us had won a bet no one had called.

And Honorable Mister was still strutting around in his stovepipe hat.

"Take a gold coin out for each of you, Jacob, and give them to me," he said. "I'll pay you all tomorrow. Each coin is worth about three hundred dollars now, I hear.

"Yes, sir," he added, "thanks to Solomon, I'm still a rich man." He smiled at my friend.

Solomon smiled, then his smile faded. That was Solomon.

"And Honorable, sir," I said, "what day is this?"

"Oh," he said, turning from the barn door. "They just told me. Today is January fifteenth. We missed it, but Merry Christmas!"

Merry Christmas and Happy Birthday to me, I thought.

Outside the midnight sky released snow like white goose down feathers from a pillow. Trees inside Fort Laramie were quilted in white for their January sleep in the territory of Wyoming. The year of our Lord was eighteen hundred and sixty-one, and the president-elect was Mr. Abraham Lincoln. I wrote all this in my Book of Life.

For us freed slaves, in spite of winter's blast of western cold, the times blew apple-blossom warm. As Mama had said, "We be saved by hope."

AUTHOR'S NOTE

The turbulent 1850s and 1860s were times of decision for slavery. After the Mexican War of 1846–48 America gained all or parts of California, Nevada, Utah, Arizona, and New Mexico. Under the Compromise of 1850, designed by Stephen Douglas, Henry Clay, Daniel Webster, and others, California entered the Union as a free state. However, other states and territories had "squatter sovereignty," or the right to vote to decide whether to be a slave or a free state.

With that Compromise of 1850, there was a new federal law regarding the return of runaway slaves. This supported the Fugitive Slave Law of 1793, which had been largely ignored in the North. There were penalties for anyone who aided a slave's escape and punishment for anyone who interfered with the recovery of a slave.

In 1857 the Supreme Court announced in the Dred Scott decision that even when a slave was in a free state, the master-slave relationship remained valid. Since slaves moving into free states with owners remained slaves, and since settlers were moving to the West, the distinction between slave and free states hardly existed. The Court also declared that slavery could not be kept out of the territories, denouncing the Missouri Compromise.

From 1820 onward the Missouri Compromise had allowed states to come into the Union peacefully, because only those states below thirty-six degrees latitude could allow slavery. That compromise had foreseen a future lessening of slavery. But the California Compromise and the Kansas-Nebraska Act allowed new states to decide to adopt or to reject slavery for themselves.

Illinois lawyer Abraham Lincoln was disturbed by the possible extension of slavery. In 1852 Harriet Beecher Stowe wrote *Uncle Tom's Cabin,* a powerful influence when acted out in small-town plays; and Lincoln's law partner was a strong abolitionist. These are factors that might have influenced Lincoln.

During the election campaign for the Illinois senatorial seat in 1858, a position then held by Stephen Douglas, Lincoln gave a speech that recalled America's former "slavery" to King George of England, and he reminded his audience that the statement in the U.S. Constitution "all men are created equal" was deemed "a self-evident fact" after the U.S. victory in the Revolutionary War. But, he continued, now that the nation had grown "fat and greedy to be masters," those words had become "a self-evident lie." He doubted that the United States could continue to exist as a half-slave, half-free land, saying, "A house divided against itself cannot stand."

Although Abraham Lincoln lost the senatorial race and Stephen Douglas won a second term, the so-named House Divided speech was printed in newspapers across the country and made Lincoln a well-known figure. He had been a Whig, but he realized that he now felt more comfortable as a member of the new radical Republican Party.

Meanwhile, gold was discovered in California in 1848; both the South and the North needed gold. California, however, was three thousand miles from the capital of the United States, and news took months to reach the new state. If California's businessmen and gold were to remain in the Union, mail must reach and return from there quickly.

On the East Coast telegraph lines carried news among eastern states and west to Missouri; on the west coast the lines carried news from Sacramento to San Francisco. But between Missouri and Sacramento lay two thousand miles of plains, deserts, and mountains.

William Russell, Alexander Majors, and William Waddell owned a company that carried supplies to the West. Russell joined John Jones to create Leavenworth and Pike's Peak Express Company in 1859 to carry mail in coaches from Missouri to Colorado. In February 1860 the route was extended to California. They built rest stations and bought more mules and horses to pull the coaches. This extended enterprise was called the Central Overland California and Pike's Peak Express Company.

The Central Overland coach route took twenty-two days to traverse, encountered snow in winter, and crossed mountains and deserts. It was too far north to be seized by angry Southerners, sometimes called Fire-Eaters, who defended slavery as property.

By contrast, a route preferred by some, called the Ox-Bow or Butterfield Route, dropped down from Missouri to Arkansas, Texas, New Mexico, and Arizona and back up north to San Francisco. This southern route was two hundred miles longer, passed through unfriendly Apache and Comanche territories, and took fifty days by coach. It was also at the mercy of Southern slave owners.

By water, mail and news traveled fifteen thousand miles around Cape Horn to California and took four to six months. The Pacific Mail Steamship Line sailed the Atlantic Ocean with mail. Then carriers traveled through Panama's dangerous jungles and continued by ship on the Pacific to sail up to San Francisco.

So-called Jackass Express delivery men on mules took letters and newspapers from West Coast post offices to people in the hills panning gold at places such as Dead Man's Gulch, Murderer's Bar, and Hog's Glory.

To answer the need for rapid communication, in the spring of 1860 William Russell borrowed money and began the Pony Express. Lightweight riders carried mail and newspapers on mixed-breed mustang horses riding west from Missouri to California and east from California to Missouri.

With changes of galloping horses every ten to fifteen miles, limited loads, and changes of riders every hundred miles, mail traveled across the two thousand miles in about ten days.

Mail was carried in a large, square, leather saddle blanket called a mochila. All four corners had locked mail pouches, and the mochila had a hole for rapid attachment to the saddle horn.

When stationmasters saw the dust of a rider coming, they saddled a fresh horse from their corral to keep the delivery moving. A Pony Express rider had two minutes to leap off the horse, transfer the mochila to a fresh horse, drink, perhaps eat a mouthful, and continue galloping on his way.

In November 1860 Edward Creighton left Missouri to map a route for the telegraph to cross the country to Sacramento, California. The first poles were laid in Kansas. In the spring of 1861 the race began to dig holes, sink telegraph posts, lay wire, and build relay stations every fifty miles across the West. Only a few months after beginning, on October 26, 1861, telegraph crews from

Missouri traveling west and crews from California working their way east met in the center for a news dispatch. Now America was united from Atlantic to Pacific by the transcontinental telegraph.

The Pony Express, begun on April 3, 1860, had carried news through deep snow in the winter of 1860–61. The brave riders had survived alkali dust in the western deserts, rivers flooded in springtime, hot sun in summertime, deep snow in wintertime, outlaws, and murderers. However, after a year and a half the new telegraph system ended the need for the Pony Express. Some of its relay stations were used by the telegraph company.

In that fall and winter of 1860–61 a group calling themselves the Knights of the Golden Circle wanted California to become a separate Republic of the Pacific. Other groups wanted California to secede from the Union along with the South.

When news of Abraham Lincoln's election reached there by way of the Pony Express, the California legislature passed a resolution pledging support for the United States. The Pony Express had saved the state and its gold for the Union.

President James Buchanan's Secretary of War, John B. Floyd, secretly shipped cannons, guns, and ammunition from Springfield, Massachusetts, to California and to some Southern states. News of the conspiracy reached Missouri via the Pony Express and was telegraphed to Washington

City. President Buchanan quelled the insurrection.

After the Southern states fired on Fort Sumter in April 1861, a limited number of mail riders in local areas, along with the transcontinental telegraph, kept East and West together during the Civil War.

The Pony Express firm had been bankrupt since its beginning. William Russell never received a government contract for the mail delivery. Unfortunately, he became involved in a funding scandal. Using Interior Department bonds, he had borrowed cash to pay his Pony Express riders. As a result, Russell was arrested and sent to jail. However, with help from influential friends, he was soon released.

In *Twelve Travelers, Twenty Horses* our ten slaves and their owners are fictional, but other people in the story are historical. Jacob Israel Christmas was living in exciting times, but we also live in exciting times. Today, as in the past, children and adults must be prepared for their roles in an ever-changing world.

Bibliography

Coe, Lewis. *The Telegraph: A History*. Jefferson, North Carolina: McFarland and Company, 1993.

Godfrey, Anthony. *Historic Resource Study: Pony Express National Historic Trail*. Washington, D.C.: United States Department of the Interior, National Park Service, U.S. Government Printing Office, 1994.

Lorant, Stefan. *Lincoln: A Picture Story of His Life*. New York: Harper and Brothers, 1957.

MacLeod, Charlotte. *Brass Pounder*. Boston: Little, Brown, and Company, 1971.

Ortiz, Alfonso, ed. *Handbook of North American Indians*. Vol. 9, *Southwest*. Washington, D.C.: Smithsonian Institution, 1979.

Reinfeld, Fred. *Pony Express*. New York: Macmillan, 1966.

Rice, Lee M., and Glenn R. Vernam. *They Saddled the West*. Cambridge, Maryland: Cornell Maritime Press, 1975.

Rittenhouse, Jack D. *American Horse-Drawn Vehicles*. New York: Bonanza Books, 1948.